CALLED

A NOVEL ABOUT
YOUTH MINISTRY TRANSITION

by Jen Bradbury

CALLED

The Youth Cartel, LLC
www.theyouthcartel.com
Email: info@theyouthcartel.com
Born in San Diego
Printed worldwide

To my Jakes: Kitty, Tony, Ginny, & Bob.
You're who I have to thank for being—and staying—in ministry.

THURSDAY, APRIL 2: THE CALL

Kendall walked into her home and slammed the door. After five years of marriage, she knew her actions would get a rise out of her husband, Frank.

Sure enough, she heard Frank push his chair back from his desk in their home office directly above her head and walk the twenty-seven steps to where she stood in the kitchen, waiting for him.

"What's wrong?" Frank asked.

"It's been a day," Kendall replied, her voice far from calm.

"It seems like there's been a lot of days like that lately," agreed Frank.

"There have been. But this one might just take the cake. Jill called Nate today."

Even as Kendall said Jill's name she felt her blood boil. In many ways, Jill was a typical SAM—*Springfield Area Mom*. She dressed well, looked perfect, worked out multiple times a week, and helicoptered over her teens at every opportunity, constantly convinced that without her, their lives would fall apart.

The first time Kendall met Jill, she'd been all smiles. She'd fawned all over Kendall, saying how delighted she was to have Kendall join their "family of Grace."

The second time they'd met, Jill walked into Kendall's office with a yellow clipboard in hand and asked for a few minutes of Kendall's time. Kendall foolishly agreed, a mistake she'd vowed never to repeat.

During that meeting, Jill had addressed a list of "growing concerns" she had regarding Kendall's recent decisions about the youth ministry. Since "youth ministry is supposed to be about the *body*, soul, and heart," Jill's family was concerned about the calories in the snacks found in the youth room. She was also perturbed that some of the "cooler" kids were no longer coming to The Lighthouse, their weekly youth program. And she was *especially* anxious about the new kids who'd recently begun coming. They weren't from the "kinds of families" that usually frequented Grace, which had set off all kinds of alarm bells in Jill's mind. She feared these newcomers would introduce her beloved daughter to all kinds of sexual sin, including porn.

Kendall had found it difficult not to stare open-mouthed at Jill as she spoke, especially as she systematically checked things off the list attached to her clipboard, a list that Kendall jokingly began referring to as "Kendall's sins."

Since then, Kendall had butted heads with Jill on a regular basis. Usually, she was wise enough to try her best to steer clear of these conflicts. But sometimes, she just couldn't help herself. Other times, Jill's reactions really did catch her off guard.

As if Frank could read Kendall's mind, he questioned, "Jill's reaction isn't that surprising, is it?"

"No, it's not," replied Kendall honestly. "I had a hunch that duct-taping kids to the wall was not going to go over well with her. But you'll still never believe what she did! She asked Nate how he could continue to support a youth pastor who obviously thinks there's nothing wrong with subjecting kids to bondage."

"Bondage?" laughed Frank. "That's a new one, even for her. What did Nate tell her?"

"That's the thing," Kendall said hesitantly. "I don't know. I ran into Nate at the end of the day as I was walking out the door. He said we needed to talk because Jill had called him. He wondered why she thought I was subjecting the high school teens to bondage. I laughed until he assured me he was serious. I suggested we talk right away, but Nate said he had an evening meeting and needed to get home to Beth and the kids before then. It made me feel as though he didn't even want to hear my side of things."

"I don't think that's it at all," Frank, who always tried to see the best in people, replied calmly. "It sounds like Nate just had a busy day and he wanted to give you a heads up about what Jill said. What time are you going to meet with him tomorrow?"

"3:00," said Kendall, exasperated. "That means my whole morning is shot because I'm going to be worried about this. It's going to make it hard for me to focus on anything else."

"Don't catastrophize this, Kendall. Just go talk to Nate. This isn't the end of the world."

"Then how come it feels like it is?" Kendall cried.

Frank enveloped Kendall in a giant bear hug as she finally let her tears fall.

■ ■ ■

FRIDAY, APRIL 3: THE BLOWUP

Overnight, Kendall had her recurring nightmare, in which Jill's increasingly awful antics finally resulted in Kendall being fired from Grace.

Finally, Kendall awoke with a start, exhausted but relieved to be awake. She tiptoed down the steps and grabbed her breakfast Pepsi, hoping not to wake Frank in the process. She then retreated into the sunroom, her favorite room in their house. She sat down in her prayer chair and began her morning quiet time.

Ever since she'd begun prepping for Wednesday's lesson with her teens about the Israelites' time in slavery in Egypt, Kendall had felt drawn to their story. She couldn't explain why, especially since it was a story she knew well. And yet, as she opened her Bible to Exodus 1, not for the first time, she felt like she was reading this passage with fresh eyes.

As she read, Kendall thought about oppression. She knew that her life was good, undeniably good.

And yet.

As she read Exodus 1, she found herself substituting Jill's name in for the Egyptians and her own in place of the Israelites. So often during her years at Grace she'd felt as though Jill was her ruthless taskmaster, unfairly responding to anything and everything she did.

Oh, Kendall knew her line of thinking was dangerous. She knew many biblical hermeneutics professors who would roll over in their graves if they heard her thoughts.

But after a day like yesterday, she couldn't keep her mind from going there. She wondered how her meeting today would go and whether she'd leave seeing Nate as the Egyptians, or worse—the Pharaoh.

Kendall hoped not.

Even with as much grief as Nate had caused her, Kendall still wanted to believe he was better than a Pharaoh, maybe because when she first came to Grace, she was enamored with Nate. He said all the right things about youth ministry and the church. He was dynamic, in life and in the pulpit. She'd envisioned herself learning a ton from him and had imagined a bright future and partnership between them.

Unfortunately, in the years she'd been at Grace, Kendall's relationship with Nate had fallen far short of her dream for it. While Nate was dynamic from the pulpit, he was certainly not a dynamic, collaborative, or even fun boss. She'd given up trying to learn from him because she'd quickly realized he never had time for her unless there was a problem. Then, suddenly, he had all the time in the world for her.

At first, Kendall convinced herself that Nate's absence actually worked in her favor. It meant she had a long leash that she could do what she wanted with. But lately, she'd come to see that in this case the cliché was true: The longer her leash, the easier it was to hang herself with it.

Before Kendall's thoughts could get any more depressing, Frank wandered into the sunroom, his cup of coffee in hand. He sat down in the Ikea chair next to hers. "How are you doing?" he wondered, knowing she'd had a rough night.

She sighed audibly and then launched into a recap of everything she'd just been thinking about.

"Let's not get too far ahead of ourselves," Frank cautioned. "Nate's bad but he's not like the Pharaoh. At least not yet."

Frank chuckled to himself in a way that typically put Kendall at ease.

Today, however, neither his comments nor his laughter relaxed her. Instead, the whole situation felt ominous.

Kendall glanced at her watch, only to realize with a start that she was out of time. She had to get to work.

She ran upstairs, took a quick shower, and grabbed a pair of jeans. She bypassed the hoodie she really wanted to wear on this chilly April day in favor of a modest, professional-looking top. For better or worse, she never felt quite free enough to wear what she wanted to work. Whether it was because she was female and concerned what people would think or because she was intimidated by Nate's permanent tie, she wasn't sure.

As Kendall walked the four blocks from her house to church, she mentally prepared her day's to-do list. Since it was a Friday, she had several meetings, including her weekly staff meeting with her colleagues. She'd then have to send out her weekly email to parents, do her monthly finances, arrange a one-on-one with one of her students and one of her leaders, finish prepping Sunday's lesson, and work on her student leadership team agenda. Unfortunately, she'd have to do it all while dreading her meeting with Nate and talking about his call with Jill.

As soon as Jill entered Kendall's thoughts, she began to replay the events of the last two days, something she'd done at least a hundred times since talking to Nate the day before. She desperately kept trying to figure out what had gone so horribly wrong.

It had been a pretty average Wednesday night gathering for their high school youth ministry. About fifty high schoolers came, if not eager to learn about Jesus at least excited to hang out with each other and play games.

For their opener, Kendall divided the kids into several teams and handed each team two jumbo rolls of duct tape. She began as she always did, by saying, "Your job, should you choose to accept it…" She then launched into the goal of the game, in this case to duct-tape a person to the wall of The Lighthouse.

The teens roared in anticipation and then eagerly started working together. Much to her surprise and delight, teens actually fought one another over who got to be the person duct-taped to the wall. On more than one team, teens rock-paper-scissored one another for the honor.

By all accounts, everyone enjoyed the game. Laughter echoed throughout the gym as teams strategized, hoisted, and then frantically taped one another to the wall. Squeals from teens as they slowly slid down the wall after their duct tape failed even lured the choir in from down the hall, curious to see what was happening. Their smiles showed Kendall how delighted they were to see The Lighthouse filled with high schoolers.

Kendall made sure to snap some great pictures, which she knew they'd use on social media. Once the laughter died down and the last teen slid down the wall, she then launched into a lesson on bondage.

Hmmm, Kendall thought to herself as she walked, a light bulb suddenly turning on for her. *Maybe Jill actually got the bondage term from me.*

The more Kendall thought about it, the more she realized it wasn't much of a stretch.

She'd intentionally tied their game to their lesson, knowing that the connection to the game would make the lesson more likely to "stick" with the kids. Kendall began by giving teens time to process the game in their small groups. Together, they wrestled with questions like:

- What was it like to be (or to see someone) stuck to the wall?
- Whose fault was it that you (or someone else on your team) was stuck to the wall?
- How did it feel to stick someone to the wall?

- Whose help would you have needed to get down from the wall?

After teens returned from their small groups, Kendall then taught about how, throughout history, different groups of people have been trapped by others. She called this bondage and then walked through a brief history of slavery beginning with the Israelites' captivity in Egypt and continuing on to the African slave trade in the 1700s and 1800s, as well as into modern-day examples of slavery like sex trafficking.

At the end of the night, Kendall had felt exceptionally good about her teaching. She could tell her teens were with her throughout the night by the way they leaned toward her, eager to hear the next part of her talk, and by the questions they asked at the end of the night. After they closed with prayer and worship, several teens even stayed to ask more questions and share ideas about how they'd like to see The Lighthouse work for justice in these areas.

Kendall had gone home that night exhausted but ecstatic.

Thursday morning—the day Jill called Nate—one of Kendall's student leaders, Jonathan, posted a variety of duct-tape pictures to Instagram using the hashtag #StuckOnGod. He then gave a recap of the night's discussion.

Nothing about the post had worried Kendall, especially when she saw how many of her teens were liking and reposting it to their feeds. Unfortunately, midway through the day, she'd seen Jill comment, "Bondage! How is this an appropriate game or topic for our high school youth?"

Despite her history with Jill, Kendall thought this was yet another example of Jill oversexualizing something—in this case, the word *bondage*—and overreacting like the helicopter mom she was. Nevertheless, she'd honestly meant to give Nate a heads up.

Unfortunately, when she'd finally gotten a moment to do so, Nate had been in another meeting. Then Rachel, a sophomore whose parents were in the midst of a horrific divorce, had stopped by and Kendall had spent the rest of the afternoon ministering to her.

By the time she'd packed up her stuff and prepared to walk home, she'd forgotten all about it. Until, that is, she'd run into Nate in the hall.

Lost in her own world, Kendall was surprised when she looked up and saw the church building right in front of her. She dropped her backpack in her office and headed to the staff meeting. From there, the day passed in a blur. Despite her fears that she'd be unable to focus, Kendall's to-do lists kept her grounded until her alarm went off at 2:45 p.m.

She ducked into the bathroom and then headed down the hall, mentally composing an apology for how Jill's call had caught Nate off guard.

When Kendall got to Nate's office, she was surprised to see the door shut and hear laughter coming from inside.

She stepped forward and knocked timidly.

Nate came to the door and invited her in.

Much to Kendall's horror, as she stepped into Nate's office, she realized that the laughter she'd heard moments ago was coming from Jill, who was sitting in Nate's office, in the flesh.

Almost unconsciously, Kendall felt her hands move together as she subtly formed the sign for *awkward turtle* that she often caught her teens using in situations like this.

Despite Kendall's increasing discomfort, she fully expected Nate to usher Jill out the door.

Instead, he turned to Kendall and said, "I thought it might be helpful for us all to talk this little incident through together. Maybe then we can find a way forward. After all, we want the same things for our kids: We want them to love and follow Jesus."

Kendall pasted her best, most professional smile on her face while she sank into the chair that Nate offered her.

Inside, however, she seethed. She could not believe that Nate had invited Jill to attend this meeting, especially without warning her first.

Jill's presence felt like the epitome of betrayal. Even though this was not the first time Nate had failed to rise to her defense, she'd never felt as unsupported by him as she did in this moment. Even before anyone spoke, she had a hard time believing they'd find a way forward. Right now, she couldn't even look Nate in the eye.

Still, she sat, unflinching, as Nate spoke. "So, Jill, I just wanted to thank you for reaching out to me."

"Absolutely, Pastor!" Jill said sweetly. "I know how much you care about our congregations' teens so I just wanted to make sure you knew what happened at youth group earlier this week. I couldn't imagine that Kendall's actions would have met with your approval."

As Jill began, Kendall flashed back to the meeting she and Jill had all those years ago, with Jill's bright yellow clipboard and the list of Kendall's sins. She imagined the glee Jill must have felt at adding this most recent atrocity to her list.

Kendall fought to stay present, but found it hard as Nate nodded his head in agreement at Jill, without so much as even a glance at Kendall. "You're absolutely right. I was hugely disappointed in Kendall's lack of judgment in deciding to duct-tape teens to the wall this week. I'm sure that Kendall has an apology for you."

Nate looked at Kendall, waiting for her to begin.

Kendall sat stunned, unsure what to say.

In that instant, she flashed back to her nightmares of the previous night and realized with certainty that she was living them. This woman was about to get her fired. The realization activated Kendall's *fight* response.

"Actually, Nate," she said pointedly, "I thought it might be helpful for you both to hear what really happened. On Wednesday, fifty high schoolers from all three of our area schools joined us for youth group. The Lighthouse was full of energy. I really wish you could have seen it firsthand like some of our choir members did."

Kendall knew that had she been in a better state of mind, she might have filtered her last comment out. But she wasn't and so she didn't. In her three years of working for Nate, he'd never—not once— actually attended one of her programs to see her in action. He had no idea what went on at The Lighthouse each week. He had no idea how amazing it was that they had fifty high schoolers attending The Lighthouse each week.

Nate had no idea what she did, which Kendall was only just beginning to realize was part of the problem. She thought again of the long leash she'd been given at Grace and wondered if she was about to strangle herself with it before taking a deep breath and continuing.

"Our teens had a blast on Wednesday. They were laughing and joking and even rock-paper-scissoring each other to decide who got to be duct-taped to the wall."

"That's not what Christy said," interrupted Jill, referencing her daughter. "According to her, NO ONE wanted to play your little game of bondage."

"I hate to contradict you, Jill, but I've got ten leaders who would say otherwise. Our teens were enthusiastic about the night's game."

"In what world is it okay to duct-tape students to the wall?" questioned Jill, her temper and volume both rising.

"It was just a game, Jill," Kendall replied, as calmly as possible under the circumstances. "For what it's worth, we never force anyone to play the opening games, ever. It's always challenge-by-choice. Last week was no exception. But no one opted out."

"You know as well as I do that no one could actually opt out of your little games—even if they wanted to," Jill cried angrily. "You've got too much power! The rest of the kids would make fun of them!"

"No, they wouldn't," replied Kendall. "We work really hard at The Lighthouse to ensure that every teen is welcome and to emphasize that no one is allowed to make fun of anyone else. Kids opt out of games all the time, for a variety of reasons. But no one opted out of this one."

"Well," Jill said, "how did you decide who would be duct-taped to the wall?"

"Like I said, kids were actually battling one another for that honor," answered Kendall. "No group had a hard time finding someone. Most groups actually had a hard time deciding who NOT to duct-tape to the wall. I also think it's important to note that your daughter, Christy, was one of the students who volunteered for that privilege!"

"I know!" cried Jill, apparently forgetting she'd just claimed no one had wanted to play at all. "But that's my point. She never should have! She's heavy for her age. What if she had fallen down? She would have been the laughingstock of the junior class!"

At that moment, Kendall realized they were getting to the root of the problem. She wondered if this had been Jill's problem all along: that she was insecure about Christy and perhaps her own body image.

The realization helped give Kendall a bit of empathy toward Jill, enough to calmly reassure her.

"Christy is beautiful, on both the inside and outside. She was in no danger of falling. In fact, we had several guys—far larger than

Christy—who volunteered to be taped. Really, truly, everyone was having fun."

With that, Kendall saw Jill visibly start to relax. Unfortunately, Nate didn't. He picked that moment to interrupt. "Kendall, I don't believe I've heard you apologize for the trauma you obviously caused Christy and Jill."

Kendall's mouth fell open. Had she really just heard Nate right?

Just when they were starting to make some progress and actually enter into some productive dialogue, Nate chose this moment to ask for her apology?

She felt like she was living in an alternate reality. Had he really missed what had just happened?

Wanting to give him the benefit of the doubt, Kendall cautiously began again. "Before we get to that, Nate, I'd like to go back to what we were just talking about."

As though he were batting away a fly, Nate raised his hand and waved it at Kendall before reiterating that she needed to apologize.

Left with no other choice, Kendall swallowed what little remained of her dignity. "I'm sorry for any problems that this has caused you and Christy, Jill."

That was the most authentic apology Kendall could come up with in the moment.

As she waited for Jill to respond, Nate once again interjected. "Perhaps it would be good for you to also admit your lapse of judgment, Kendall."

"I'm sorry, Nate," retorted Kendall, as she felt the leash's hold on her neck tighten. "I can't. I don't believe I had a lapse of judgment. On Wednesday, I led a tested and tried game in the world of youth ministry. The kids had a blast—as you can clearly see from the photos Jonathan posted on Instagram. I even used this game to talk about how it feels to be stuck in our lives, trapped in any way. The teens participated so well in our conversation and teaching. They were open, honest, and incredibly vulnerable. And I've got ten other adult leaders who can attest to that."

Nate, obviously angry, cut Kendall off. "You're missing the point, Kendall. Please wait in the hall for me while I finish talking with Jill."

Kendall felt shamed, as though she were sixteen years old again, the one time she'd been called to the principal's office at her high school for cheating to get through a trig test she'd forgotten about—except this time she hadn't even done anything wrong.

Kendall looked at Nate, willing him to change his mind and say something, anything, that would make this moment better.

He didn't. Instead, he simply motioned again for Kendall to leave.

As soon as she was safely in the hallway, Kendall's tears fell. They only increased when she overheard Nate apologize to Jill and assure her that he would be taking a more active approach in supervising Kendall from here on out.

Hearing the sliding of the chairs from inside Nate's office, Kendall looked around, frantically searching for a place to hide so she wouldn't have to see Jill as she left. Finding none, she brushed her tears off with her sleeve in an effort to preserve what little was left of her dignity.

Nate passed by her, eager to walk Jill to the door.

Kendall waited, curious what would happen now that Jill was gone.

When Nate returned, he motioned for Kendall to follow him into his office.

"I can't believe you just did that, Kendall!" screamed Nate as he slammed his office door shut, as though that would keep the rest of their colleagues from overhearing.

"ME!?" yelled Kendall. "You set me up! You gave me no warning that Jill was going to be here. You asked me to come meet with you for what I thought was going to be a conversation about what actually happened."

"You completely disrespected me in front of one of our biggest supporters and givers," said Nate.

Oh, thought Kendall to herself. That explained a lot. She'd been to Jill's house before and knew it was large. She had seen the way Jill and Christy dressed. She knew Christy had gotten a brand-new car for her sixteenth birthday, and not a cheap one, since Frank constantly joked it was his dream car. Even so, she'd never guessed Jill's family was a big giver at Grace.

Nate was so worked up he seemed unable or unwilling to take a breath. "If you want to work here, you've got to show me and those in our congregation that you respect me. I am the senior pastor here. You are not. Your job is to have MY BACK. It's to make me look good. It's to keep crap like this off my desk, not pile it on. Your job is to make my life easier, not harder."

Caught completely off guard, Kendall hurriedly looked at the ceiling, hoping to blink back the tears she feared would start falling again.

She willed herself to find some empathy for Nate. She wondered why he was reacting so harshly to this situation. It seemed so disproportionate. But she didn't dare ask. That just wasn't the kind of relationship they had.

Kendall chose her words carefully. "I'm sorry, Nate. I thought my job was to disciple teens and to help them become lifelong followers of Jesus."

"Of course it is," snapped Nate. "But you have to learn how to do that in a way that reflects positively on our church and its leadership. Instagramming pictures of the kids duct-taped to the wall does NOT do that."

"Again, I'm sorry," pleaded Kendall, hoping to break Nate from whatever sort of fury-induced haze he seemed to be in.

As though she'd never spoken, Nate continued. "You need to write an apology to Jill and Christy. You also need to write a public apology to The Lighthouse community that will appear in next week's e-blast."

"I'm not sure I can do that," replied Kendall honestly.

"Sure you can," said Nate. "Just assure parents you had a lapse in judgment that will not happen again."

Kendall nodded slowly, still trying not to make Nate any angrier than he already was, convinced that things could not get any worse. But as she tried to convince herself of that, Nate continued. "And just to make sure you don't have any more judgment lapses, from here on out you need to approve your lesson plan with me each week. I need to sign off on your game AND your teaching."

"You're going to micromanage me now?" Kendall was incredulous.

Kendall's long leash had been what she'd clung to. It was her reason for staying at Grace, despite her mounting frustrations with Nate. Every time she thought about looking for a new job, she replayed the horror stories from her fellow youth workers about what it was like to work for micromanagers. If her freedom disappeared, she didn't know why else she'd stay.

Feeling as though she could hardly make things worse at this point, Kendall found her voice. "This is your solution to one negative parent? I can't believe that this is how you treat your staff. No wonder no youth pastor has ever worked for you longer than a year! You can't treat people like this!"

No sooner had the words come out of Kendall's mouth than she regretted them. Sure, they were true. Prior to her time there, Grace had had a new youth pastor every year for the previous six. But as hard as Nate was to work for, Kendall had never actually blamed him for their exits. She knew that churches were complicated systems and that each one of those youth pastors had undoubtedly contributed to their own short tenure here as well.

At least that's what she'd always told herself.

Now she wasn't so sure.

Kendall was trying to figure out what to say to make everything better when Nate glared at her and continued. "As we've already established, Kendall, I am the senior pastor at Grace. You are merely the youth pastor. You are expendable. I hired you and let me assure you, I can fire you—anytime I want to. As you just alluded to yourself, I've done it before. I think we're done here. I'll expect to see your apology on my desk first thing on Monday as well as your lesson plan for Wednesday."

"And if I refuse?" Kendall asked quietly.

"Then you can give me your resignation instead," retorted Nate. "Any other questions, Kendall?"

Kendall shook her head no, shocked by what had just transpired. She stood and fled the room.

Back in her office, Kendall called Frank and told him everything that had just happened, crying as she did.

"Frank?" she questioned, shortly after finishing. "You still there?"

There was a pause before he responded. "I'm here. I just have no words. Nate has never been the best boss for you, but this time his actions have left me speechless. What are you going to do?"

"I don't know," Kendall sobbed into the phone. "I'm not sure I can work for Nate after that. But I also feel no sense of release from my ministry here at Grace. I can apologize to Jill if that's what it takes to keep my job… But if I do that, am I betraying myself? I really don't feel like I did anything wrong."

"You didn't, sweetie," said Frank reassuringly.

"You have to say that," Kendall quickly replied. "You're married to me."

"Even if I wasn't I would say the same thing. Nate was out of line here. Maybe you should call Jake," suggested Frank, referring to Kendall's longtime mentor and friend. Jake had been in youth ministry for twenty-five years, at three different churches. "Hasn't he always told you that when you feel like you're getting ready to jump off a cliff—or, in this case, get pushed off a cliff—you should call him?"

Although Frank couldn't see it, Kendall nodded her head, thinking of all the other times in their relationship when Jake had indeed kept her from jumping. It seemed like that's what Jake had been doing ever since they met when she and Frank were in college. Jake was the youth pastor at their college church, where both she and Frank served in the youth ministry. During Kendall's senior year, Jake had consistently called out Kendall's gifts. He'd given her opportunities to explore youth ministry and then encouraged her to consider pursuing a job as a youth pastor rather than using her business degree.

After much wrestling with God, Kendall realized she was indeed being called into ministry. Jake had been her number one cheerleader ever since. He'd helped her to land her first job in ministry and had coached, mentored, and guided her in the years since, including when she'd transitioned to Grace.

Realizing how much she needed her mentor, she hastily hung up the phone with Frank, confident he'd be glad she did. She called Jake, filled him on everything that had transpired, and then arranged to meet him at their normal coffee spot the next morning. As she hung up, she thought again how fortunate she was that Jake had relocated to their area not long after she and Frank had moved to Springfield.

Despite her tumultuous day, Kendall hoped that merely knowing she and Jake would meet tomorrow would be enough to ensure her a good night's sleep.

It wasn't.

■ ■ ■

SATURDAY, APRIL 4: THE ADVICE

After a restless night of sleep, Kendall finally deemed it an acceptable hour to stop tossing and turning. Before getting out of bed, she rolled over and shook Frank's shoulders. "Tell me something good," she begged as he looked at her groggily.

"Oh, baby. There's so much good. I know this sucks. But we are going to get through this. Team Kendall and Frank always comes out on top. You are unbelievably good at this work you do. In fact, you're so good that sometimes I wonder if Nate actually feels threatened. Jake's going to give you some good advice this morning and then we'll work through it and decide what's next. You can do this."

Buoyed by Frank's words and the thought of caffeine, Kendall got ready, then headed out the door and drove to The Perk to meet Jake.

"It is *so* good to see you, friend," Kendall said as she fell into Jake's warm, reassuring hug. She felt her whole posture change.

"I bet," said Jake. "It sounds like you've had a pretty rough few days. Let's go grab some coffee, my treat."

Kendall smiled appreciatively and walked up to the counter. Jake ordered his usual, a tall black coffee, while Kendall got a grande caramel macchiato, extra whip. While they waited for their orders, the two chatted amicably about Frank and about Jake's wife and three kids.

When they sat back down, Kendall was relieved she'd filled Jake in on what had happened yesterday during their call. The thought of reliving it all again felt absolutely exhausting.

Jake looked at her, silently inviting Kendall to begin talking.

"You always said ministry was hard, Jake," began Kendall. "But when you said it, I assumed you meant that actual *ministry* was hard… you know, working with teens and walking with them through tough stuff. But that's a piece of cake compared to juggling church politics, working for people like Nate, and dealing with parents like Jill. After yesterday, I'm not sure I want to keep going. I'm not sure I *can* keep going."

"Oh, Kendall," said Jake in a way that soothed her weary soul. "I hear you. I've been there. But you cannot quit on your worst day. That's not fair to you, the church, or your teens."

"But what if this isn't my worst day?" wondered Kendall aloud. "What if I stay at Grace and things just keep getting worse and worse?"

Kendall imagined a situation in which instead of just Jill causing problems, there was a whole army of angry parents actively working against her… Or a situation in which her leaders suddenly turned on her… Or a situation in which her ministry stopped bearing fruit… Or a situation in which her budget got slashed, even more than it already had been.

After almost six years in ministry, Kendall knew that any of these things—or all of them—could actually happen. That thought scared her. A lot. Especially since based on her experience at Grace she doubted Nate would support her in any of those scenarios. She worried that eventually, Nate would decide the most important goal of the youth ministry was to placate parents.

Even now, Kendall worried they weren't actually far from that. His words to Jill yesterday affirmed it.

Before her thoughts could stray any further, Jake interrupted. "You're right, Kendall. Things might actually get worse. I can't promise you they won't. I wish I could, but we both know that's not possible. So, let's talk through this."

Kendall motioned for Jake to continue, which, thankfully, he did.

"I spent a lot of time last night thinking about your conversation with Nate. Nate abused your trust in so many ways. He asked you to attend a meeting that you weren't prepared for. He intentionally sideswiped you by inviting Jill without telling you. Unfortunately, it's not the first time he's betrayed your trust, either."

Kendall knew Jake was right. This wasn't the first time Nate had betrayed her trust. He'd done so not even three months into her call to Grace.

Because Kendall had started at Grace in May, she had immediately led their summer trips. On their high school mission trip, a group of the "cool" rising seniors snuck out of the church they were staying in. Bert, one of the men whose houses they'd been painting, found them in the Walmart parking lot late that night. Bert brought them back to the church rather than call the police, leaving Kendall to deal with them as she saw fit.

Once the teens were safely back in their rooms, Kendall gathered her trip leaders to decide how to handle the situation. She had ideas as to what needed to happen, but as a new youth pastor at the church she knew better than to make a unilateral decision. Together, she and her leaders decided to call the parents of the teens involved to let them know what happened. Unless those parents felt strongly against it, they wanted the teens to stay for the rest of the trip, as long as they apologized to the rest of the team for their actions and worked to turn their attitudes around.

Kendall and her other leaders believed strongly that this was a moment where they should extend grace to these "cool" teens. Up to this point, they had made it abundantly clear they did not want to be on the trip, which they said they'd only agreed to go on because they liked Kendall's predecessor better than her. Because they'd said that outright, Kendall was convinced they'd snuck out hoping to get sent home. Kendall thought maybe grace would actually transform these teens…and that if it didn't, staying on the trip would be worse than any other punishment she could come up with.

As Kendall suspected, grace transformed them in a way that nothing else would have. By the end of the trip, these "cool" kids had become leaders—leaders who went on to serve The Lighthouse well throughout their senior year in high school.

Of course, all Kendall knew was how well the teens had responded to the grace her team showed them on the trip. She felt great about how she and her team had weathered her first true test of leadership.

Unfortunately, she had failed to consider two things:

1. What might happen when the parents of the kids not directly involved found out about what she'd done, *and*

2. How Nate might react if he disagreed with her decision.

Sure enough, once Kendall and her team arrived home, the parents of the "cool" teens were enamored with Kendall. They could not believe the transformation in their teens.

However, the parents of those kids NOT involved in the situation were furious. They could not believe that Kendall would allow teens engaging in such risky behavior to remain on the trip. They were convinced their actions must have put everyone in danger.

Nate was livid because Kendall failed to inform him of any of this until after they returned home—when he heard it about it not from the parents of the kids actually involved, but from those who weren't. Not surprisingly, Nate took the angry parents' side, citing a covenant the team had signed prior to Kendall's arrival saying that anyone caught doing anything illegal or sneaking out would be sent home at their parents' expense. In Nate's estimation, Kendall should have followed the rules.

To this day, Kendall thought she might have...if only someone had bothered to tell her what they were.

Jake snapped his fingers in front of Kendall's face.

"Earth to Kendall," Jake said. "You still here?"

When Kendall explained to Jake what she'd been thinking about, Jake smiled knowingly. "That's exactly the instance I was referring to... Although you and I both know there have been others."

Kendall nodded in agreement.

"Like I was saying," continued Jake, "Nate has never actually been very supportive of you or your ministry. From the stories you've told, it sounds like his primary concern has always been appeasing those with power in your congregation and protecting his image. Is that really the kind of person you want to work for?"

"Of course not!" exclaimed Kendall. "But what choice do I have? You might not remember this, but I do. I applied to over twenty jobs in youth ministry. When you're female, your options are a little more limited than when you're a cool male wearing skinny jeans."

"Don't you dare go after my skinny jeans!" Jake cried, motioning toward his trademark black pair. "Your point is fair. You *did* apply to a lot of jobs and you might have to again, but you've also got three more years of experience than you did then. Plus, you've lasted longer at Grace than *either* of us thought you would. How much longer can you really work for Nate?"

"I don't know," muttered Kendall, feeling increasingly confused.

Trying to help her out, Jake continued. "It doesn't seem like Nate's someone with a lot of vision, or really, even someone with a lot of integrity. I can't help but wonder what God might do with your ministry if you were unleashed into an environment where you could really flourish, Kendall. Imagine how God might use you then!"

"But that's just it, Jake," started Kendall. "God has used me here at Grace."

Kendall's mind flashed to the fruit she'd experienced at Grace. She thought about how reluctant teens were to trust her when she'd first arrived. After the revolving door of youth pastors who came before her, teens didn't want to take time to get to know yet another person who was just going to leave. But when the teens heard and saw what she did to the "cool" teens who snuck out on the mission trip, they were intrigued enough to give her a chance. After months of showing up for her teens on their turf and going on more ice cream dates than was actually healthy, Kendall made strides.

Kendall knew a lot of the strides she'd made were also due to the leadership team she'd built. She'd invited many of the adults from her first mission trip to continue serving for the next year. Most of them did, in large part because they were curious what would become of that cool group of seniors. During their year together, Kendall trained and developed these adult leaders, invested in them, and thanked them. As time passed, she celebrated with them when they got married, found new jobs, and had babies. And she wept with them at more than one funeral for their parents. Much to her delight, most of those leaders were still serving with her today. She knew that a lot of her fruit was thanks to them. She also hoped that when it was time for her to leave, these leaders would continue serving without her in a way that would help continue to build trust with their teens.

And then there were the teens at The Lighthouse. Kendall loved them dearly. They were curious and many of them were wicked funny. Over the last two years in particular, their faith had really exploded. The topics they were addressing now were exponentially deeper than those they tackled her first year. And their questions… They were honest and mature, searching for Jesus at every turn.

Jake interrupted Kendall's thoughts. "You were thinking about the fruit you've seen, weren't you?"

Kendall smiled. Jake knew her so well. "I was."

"What do you notice about all the fruit your ministry has borne, Kendall?" Jake asked.

"What do you mean?"

"I mean, who's in the picture?"

"Huh?" replied Kendall, genuinely confused.

"Is Nate in the picture?" clarified Jake.

"Oh," said Kendall with a start. "No, he's not."

"Here's why that's important to remember," Jake said, his voice filled with wisdom and compassion. "Your ministry has been bearing fruit *in spite* of your relationship with Nate, not because of it. It'll *always* be hard to leave those you've worked most closely with. That'll actually only get harder the *longer* you stay. But I'd also argue you're not abandoning them. You've been at Grace for three years. That's way longer than anyone else has stayed under Nate's leadership. What if, in order to continue growing, your teens *need* someone else to lead them? Someone else who might work better with Nate?"

"Ha!" laughed Kendall. "Well, if that's what you're suggesting then I know I'm not supposed to go anywhere. Six youth pastors in six years, remember? No one is going to flourish under Nate's leadership. If I leave, I'm setting these kids up for another string of short-term youth pastors."

"But whose problem is that?"

Kendall groaned inwardly. This was one of Jake's favorite processing questions to ask. It helped her think through when she did and did not actually need to worry about something.

"Not mine," she responded honestly. "But you and I both know that long-term ministry is best, Jake. You're the one who's always told me that it takes three years before you can really accomplish anything in youth ministry. The first year, you're too busy learning the ropes. The second year, you're fighting all the fires that suddenly crop up after the honeymoon ends. The third year, you're finally able to begin building your own team. That's when the good fruit really starts growing!"

"We've known each other too long," retorted Jake with a grin. "You can't quote me back to me."

"Pretty sure I just did, you old man," laughed Kendall. "But seriously, Jake. I feel like I've seen fruit all along but there's a different kind of sweetness to this third year. Not with Nate so much, but definitely in my ministry itself. Given that, it feels surreal to even be having this conversation. How can I be thinking about leaving? I mean, how do I know when it's time?"

"You don't, Kendall. You won't. But here's a question I think you really need to wrestle with: Are you still feeling called to your role at Grace?"

"Jake," started Kendall hesitantly. "You know I respect your wisdom. But that question feels like such a copout to me. Sometimes I can't help but wonder if a calling is even real."

"Oh, a calling is real, Kendall," said Jake. "You and I both believe that. But you're right, sometimes we use the word *call* to simply justify what we feel or want. For the record, I don't think you're doing that. If anything, I think you might have overstayed your call."

"Overstayed?" asked Kendall incredulously. "I don't even understand how you can make that argument! My third year isn't even quite over!"

"But I think a lot of people wouldn't have lasted more than a year at Grace. You've faced obstacle after obstacle in your ministry and yet you're still there. I can't help but wonder if you're staying because you're afraid no one else will hire you or because you actually feel called to Grace."

"A little bit of both, I suppose," admitted Kendall.

"If you're really called to ministry, another church *will* hire you. That is, in fact, the nature of being called. When a church calls you, a search committee votes to hire you. They literally pick up the phone and call you. That's the nature of a true calling. It's not just about what you think and feel. It's about another group affirming that you have the gifts and skills needed to do a job."

"So how do I know if I'm still called to Grace?"

"Perhaps you need to test that notion out a while. Maybe it's time for you to actually put yourself out there. Dust off your resume. Look at the job banks. See if there are any youth ministry positions right now that pique your interest. Then submit your resume. I'm confident you'll get some interviews. Take them. Start seeing what possibilities there are for you. And when—not if—you actually get a job offer, you can choose. You can choose to stay at Grace or you can choose to leave and go somewhere else. But either way, you'll have a choice to make. You won't feel stuck. You won't be living out of fear that no one else will hire you."

"Well, that sounds both terrifying and liberating. Thanks for the idea. But what should I do about Nate right now? How can I get through this latest crisis?"

"I've been thinking about that ever since you called. I know that what happened was incredibly painful for you—"

"Humiliating is more accurate," interrupted Kendall.

"Humiliating then," conceded Jake. "But I wonder, what truth can you find in what Nate and Jill said to you?"

"What truth can I find?!" Kendall was incredulous. "You've already admitted that Nate was way out of line. Now you want me to find truth in what he said? I'm not sure I can."

"That's fair," replied Jake. "But I think you can. You're the epitome of a leader, and leaders are fundamentally learners. So, if truth is too painful—or rather, humiliating—a word to apply to this situation, let me ask the question differently. What have you learned from what happened, especially about yourself?"

Kendall sat silently, taken aback. This was her mentor and trusted friend. She never expected Jake to ask this of her. She'd expected him to wholly side with her.

Jake continued. "Hear me out. I'm on your side. Always have been. Always will be. But I think it's important for you to look for the nugget of truth—especially in difficult conversations. And if it makes you feel better, I think your ability to do so makes you a way better person than Nate."

"Sure," Kendall grumbled good-naturedly. "Appeal to my competitive nature to get me to do something I don't want to do. Give me a second here to think."

Jake began singing the annoying song from Jeopardy used to let people know that time was ticking.

"Really?" grinned Kendall, after enduring it for as long as she could. "I think the nugget of truth is that maybe I do sometimes get carried away with the games. I see other youth groups do the same ones, and they always look so fun! But sometimes I don't think through whether or not teens can really opt out while saving face."

"Good," encouraged Jake. "That's really good, Kendall. So, here's what I wonder. What would happen if you went back to Nate with that? What would happen if—rather than give him the apology he's after— you instead gave him your learning…and an honest commitment to do better with games? Would that feel authentic to you?"

"It would," agreed Kendall. "Way more than offering an apology that I don't really mean."

Kendall paused for a second. "But Nate is stubborn. What if it's not enough? What if he insists on the apology? What if he still forces me to get his approval on my lesson plans?"

Jake considered for a moment. "Well, if he does, we'll deal with that then. But let's see what happens first. Sound good?"

"Yep," agreed Kendall. "Thanks, Jake. Thanks for believing in me, challenging me, and continuing to guide me. I assume I can call you when the next crisis comes?"

"You know you can," said Jake. "But maybe we shouldn't let it get that far. How about if we just agree to meet next week. Same time, same place?"

"That'd be perfect."

"And Kendall," said Jake as he stood up and started to gather his things, "if you feel like you're getting ready to jump off a cliff before then, please call me. Okay?"

"Yep," grinned Kendall. "I know Frank really appreciates that too… Less processing for him to do with me after I get home."

Kendall and Jake embraced and headed out the door. On the drive home, Kendall couldn't help but say a prayer of thanksgiving, grateful for the ways that Jake continued investing in her.

Back at home, Kendall headed back to her beloved sunroom with her laptop and Pepsi. She immediately went to the job bank she kept bookmarked. Although she hadn't applied for any youth ministry jobs during the time she'd been at Grace, she'd often looked. Sometimes she saw nothing of interest. Other times she saw things that were intriguing, but didn't apply for fear of being rejected. Sometimes she felt like a traitor for even looking. Other times she was surprised she'd lasted this long at Grace. Sometimes she felt herself begin to dream about the possibility of starting over someplace new. Other times she thought it was far more wise to stay with the devil she knew than discover one she was less familiar with.

Today, though, Kendall tried to lay all her conflicting emotions aside. She thought again about what Jake had said about the power of choice and as she scrolled the job bank, she found herself reading with a different lens, with a newfound desire to actually see what was out there and what God might be calling her to.

After a couple hours spent searching multiple job banks, Kendall had earmarked five different positions she was genuinely intrigued by.

She updated her resume and found that the mere act of doing so was freeing. After distilling her three years at Grace into catchy but true phrases, she realized she had far more experience than she'd given herself credit for. Maybe she was more hirable than she thought.

One by one she tailored her cover letter to each job description, paused for a moment to collect herself, and hit send. After submitting the fifth application, she leaned back contentedly, just as Frank walked in.

"How'd it go with Jake?" he asked.

"It was good," replied Kendall. "But I suspect you know that."

"I thought it might be," said Frank. "What have you been up to? I thought I heard you come in a while ago, but I was in the middle of coding and didn't want to stop before I finished the section I was working on."

"I've been applying for jobs," Kendall said with a grin.

"Excuse me?" replied Frank. "Got something you want to share with me?"

Kendall filled Frank in on Jake's theory regarding the power of choice.

"I don't know if anything will actually come of this," Kendall assured Frank. "But it already feels so good just to have taken matters into my own hands. I feel liberated, more free than I've felt in months. Even if nothing really changes, it feels like I'm taking control of my future."

As Kendall spoke, she noticed that Frank's body language change. His jovial smile morphed into something of a scowl.

"You okay?" Kendall asked.

Frank stared at Kendall before finally speaking. "You're applying for jobs, Kendall? Like, you actually sent in your resume?"

"Yeah," replied Kendall, unsure what the problem was.

"You didn't think it'd be good for us to have a conversation about this first?"

"Oh," said Kendall, sheepishly. She'd just assumed that, after how increasingly frustrated she'd been at Grace, Frank would be happy about the prospect of leaving. She told him as much.

"I know things have been really tough at Grace the last few days and I certainly want you to be happy," muttered Frank. "But I also want you to talk to me. Not *after* you unilaterally decide to do something, but before. If we're truly a team, you can't just expect me to support you in whatever you decide when that decision has implications for me as well. I mean, where are these jobs you're applying to? Would we have to move? Are you talking about relocating?"

Kendall parsed her words carefully before responding. "You're right," she began. "I'd be really upset if you applied for jobs without telling me first and this absolutely has implications for you. I found five youth ministry jobs that I thought sounded doable. All full-time. All focused on high school, but some with a bit of middle school responsibilities. None of them would *require* us to move but one of them is in Capitol City—which is far enough away that it might be nice to move. I didn't think you'd necessarily mind that. Since you work from home, you can work from anywhere!"

Frank nodded. "That's true but it doesn't mean that I want you deciding to move without telling me. I happen to like where we live. But even if I hated it, my parents are getting older. I think it's important that we stay close to them."

"Absolutely," agreed Kendall. She hesitated a moment, debating what to say next. She knew this conversation was important but she sure didn't want to further upset Frank.

"So are you okay with my applying for these jobs?" asked Kendall, finally.

"Would it matter if I wasn't?" blurted Frank.

"I was hoping you wouldn't ask me that," Kendall said with a sigh.

"It's kind of an important question, don't you think?"

"It is," admitted Kendall. "I think I'd keep trying to convince you why it's important for me to look. I might even ask you to talk to Jake so you could hear his advice firsthand. In the end, though, if you really don't want me to apply, I won't. You matter more to me than my ministry."

"Thanks, Kendall," said Frank. "I need to hear you say that sometimes, because it doesn't always feel that way."

"I'm sorry," repeated Kendall, wisely choosing not to say anything else.

"I'm okay with you applying for these jobs," said Frank reluctantly. "Just don't relegate me to an afterthought as we continue through this process, okay?"

"I promise." She stood up and went to him. "Can we still do our date day or do you need some time?"

"I think we definitely need our date day," replied Frank. "Plus, I want to hear more about these churches you applied to work at."

That afternoon, Kendall and Frank hiked and gardened, talked, and caught up on their weeks. Kendall told Frank all about the churches she'd sent her resume to. As Frank listened to Kendall, he gave her his honest assessment of them, sharing which he'd be most interested to learn more about as well.

For dinner, Frank smoked a pork tenderloin, which they ate as they enjoyed a movie together. That night, Kendall slept well. Really well.

■ ■ ■

SUNDAY, APRIL 5: A FAIRLY NORMAL DAY

Sunday passed in its usual blur.

Kendall was up early to lead a discussion with the high schoolers. Sunday morning usually averaged about half the kids they had during the week, but she loved it because the kids who came really wanted to be there. That made the discussion get deep, fast.

They were currently in the middle of a series on the trustworthiness of the Bible. Kendall had led the series once before at one of her old congregations, and she knew it was one worth repeating. Teens always wondered how the Bible came to be and whether or not you could believe in it.

This time around, she'd found that some of her typical apologetic answers were no longer working. So, Kendall was reworking her series to explore the different types of literature found in the Bible, how to read those different types of literature, and how the Bible was canonized.

This was the third week of the series and she'd found the teens' engagement to be high. They were asking good questions, and they were truly wrestling with important questions, ones that she knew would continue to influence them as people of faith as they grew older. Today, they'd discussed some of the Old Testament history books and the room had been abuzz as teens tried to discern whether or not "historical" and "literal" were synonymous. Afterward, a sophomore girl, Caden, approached her.

"Kendall," Caden began, "I heard my parents talking the other night. They were freaked out about our Sunday morning topic. They're worried I'm going to decide the Bible's not trustworthy. But this series is doing just the opposite for me. I can't stop thinking about what we're discussing. For the first time in my life, I feel like I can really rely on what Scripture says. I've started reading very differently now that I'm understanding that you're not supposed to read Joshua the same way you read the Psalms and you're not supposed to read the Psalms the same way you read Matthew. That's been really helpful. I just wanted you to know."

Without waiting for a response, Caden turned and marched out of The Lighthouse, surrounded by a posse of her friends.

Kendall stood in awe for a minute, silently relishing Caden's words, especially after what had felt like such a tumultuous week.

"Fruit," she thought to herself. "That's the fruit that my ministry is bearing here."

She was still thinking about that fruit as she vacuumed up the Cheeto crumbs that had been ground into the carpet by the savage beasts that are teenagers on a Sunday morning. As she worked, Kendall silently prayed for Caden and for the rest of the teens who were present that morning. She emptied the vacuum bag into the trash, flipped off the lights, and then headed into the sanctuary for worship.

She was, as usual, five minutes late, but that didn't prevent her from stopping to chat with Caden's parents when she saw them in the Gathering Place outside the sanctuary. Kendall asked them about their week and shared how much she'd enjoyed Caden's contribution to the morning's discussion. Caden's parents seemed surprised to hear this. "It's clear how much Caden values her faith," Kendall said. "She's asking such good questions and really searching for understanding. You guys are doing a great job discipling Caden."

Kendall said her goodbyes and headed into worship. She found Frank sitting in their normal pew, about halfway up the pulpit side of the sanctuary. Not surprisingly, he was surrounded by what they affectionately called "church orphans," the teens who valued worship enough to attend on a Sunday morning, even if the rest of their family couldn't (or, sometimes, wouldn't).

Frank knew the kids at Grace and had a good rapport with them, in part because when she'd first begun serving at Grace, he'd been one of her regular leaders. That was how Frank had actually met two of his best friends, Pete and Andy. As Frank's work stress had increased over the last year, he'd gradually faded out, preferring to simply invest in the teens he saw on Sunday mornings.

As she walked toward their pew, Kendall was pleased to notice Rachel, the girl whose parents were divorcing, sitting in their pew. Though Rachel had been a regular fixture on Wednesday nights and Sunday morning youth group, Kendall could not recall ever seeing her in church before. She uttered a prayer of thanks to God.

"Got room for me here, Jonathan?" Kendall asked. Jonathan was her senior student leader whose Instagram post had started the whole ruckus with Jill.

"Absolutely!" he said with a grin, scooching over in the pew to make room.

As Kendall sat down, Frank signed "I love you," something they'd started doing years ago that she loved during moments like this.

In the sanctuary, squashed into a pew with a dozen teens and her husband, Kendall was immediately at peace, reminded of why she did this sacred but crazy work.

That morning, Kendall belted out the words to the songs. She prayed, asking God for a special measure of grace to be able to encounter God through Nate's sermon, despite their problems from the last week.

When the sermon began, Kendall immediately noticed Nate's trademark Scripture-themed tie. This week it was a burning bush, worn especially to connect with his sermon on Exodus 3.

Until a few minutes ago, Kendall hadn't even realized Nate was beginning a new sermon series today on the Israelites. She laughed, amazed by God's timing.

That's one way to break through my wall with Nate, she thought to herself. Here was a section of Scripture she'd felt drawn to recently. And here was Nate, talking specifically about calling, the very thing she and Jake had wrestled with the day before.

Kendall listened, intrigued by the concept of holy ground, especially since Nate kept focusing on how Moses was going about his ordinary business when he stumbled upon it. Kendall wondered if this meant it was possible to miss holy ground. In particular, she wondered if it was possible for her to miss the holy ground and God's calling.

As if anticipating her question, Nate continued. "Now for those of you wondering if it's possible to miss your calling, to miss seeing your burning bush, let me assure you, the answer is *no*. In the midst of Moses's ordinary routine, this was a sight so unusual that it compelled him to *stop*. Friends, when God wants our attention, God will get our attention, just like God got Moses's attention."

Kendall wondered if perhaps the incident with Nate and Jill was, in a strange way, her burning bush moment—the unmistakable instance God used to get her attention and jar her out of her complacency at Grace. Because that's what she was starting to feel like it was: complacency.

She found it amusing that perhaps God was, in this very moment, using Nate's own words to convince her to leave Grace.

For the rest of the sermon, Kendall stayed focused. As Nate preached, she also found herself watching the people of Grace. They were riveted by Nate, almost spellbound. She was reminded how gifted a preacher he was. His integration of personal stories with the text and current events was masterful, ensuring that what he said was timely and relevant in the lives of the parishioners.

And as always, Nate's sermon taught her something and challenged her. This week, she hadn't necessarily wanted it to. But it did. In fact, now that Kendall thought about it, Nate's sermons *always* did. They always brought new insights to old texts.

By the time the sermon ended, Kendall felt buoyed. Despite the tumultuous events of the last week, she was reminded that she did, in fact, respect Nate. He was a gifted pastor—eloquent from the pulpit and caring toward his parishioners.

There were times, like today, that she did actually want to work for him.

She just hoped she'd remember that when she headed to his office the next morning to talk more about the duct-taping incident.

■ ■ ■

MONDAY, APRIL 6: THE FOLLOW-UP

Monday morning dawned bright and sunny, a direct contradiction to Kendall's mood.

Kendall awoke feeling every bit of the weight of the conversation she was about to have with Nate. She knew that Nate was expecting her to walk in with either an apology or a resignation. But after her conversation with Jake, she wasn't prepared to offer either. That made her nervous…very nervous.

Kendall gave a cursory glance at her beloved hoodie before throwing on jeans and another professional top. The smell of bacon and eggs lured her downstairs where she found Frank at the stove.

"I figured you could use a good breakfast to get you through this morning," Frank said, throwing some shredded cheddar onto the scrambled eggs. "How are you feeling?"

"Like I'm going to throw up," Kendall replied as she grabbed her breakfast Pepsi. "But boy does everything look good. I was thinking I'd just skip breakfast this morning until I smelled this deliciousness!"

"Eat up," Frank said, passing her a plate of scrambled eggs, bacon, and sausage.

"I got these for you, too," he added, setting an old-fashioned glazed donut from Stan's on the side of Kendall's plate.

"You sure know my weakness!" Kendall exclaimed with a grin.

"That I do!" agreed Frank. "So, have you decided what you're going to say today?"

"I'm going to take Jake's advice," said Kendall between bites. "I'm not offering an apology or a resignation. But I am going to share what I've learned and see if Nate and I can find some common ground and a way to move forward."

"That sounds like a great example of taking the high road. I'm proud of you."

"Thanks, babe," said Kendall, with her mouth only slightly too full. She finished the last few bites of egg, then grabbed a paper towel and carefully wrapped her donut in it. "I'll eat this on the walk over but I've gotta run. You know how Nate hates it when I'm late."

On her walk to church, Kendall munched on her donut and prayed for the conversation she was about to have. By the time she got to Grace, her treat was gone and she felt ready to meet with Nate. Or at least as ready she'd ever be.

She stopped by her office first, then called down to Nate's office. After three years at Grace, she'd finally figured out how to place an internal call. Nate answered after the first ring, "Is now a good time?"

"It sure is," said Nate. "Why don't you come to my office?"

"I'll be right there," responded Kendall. She couldn't help but wonder why Nate never came to *her* office. It felt like a power play, especially as she processed the feelings of PTSD from her last meeting in Nate's office, where she'd been surprised by Jill.

Thankfully, only Nate was waiting for her. She slowly released the breath she'd been holding.

Nate got up to greet her and then motioned for her to sit in the chair across from his desk, which was loaded with papers and books. Kendall noted Nate's cowboy boots, which matched today's rodeo tie.

"Do you have something for me?" Nate asked.

"I don't," replied Kendall.

"Excuse me?" Nate was visibly perturbed.

"As you might expect," began Kendall, "I did a lot of thinking and praying over the weekend, and I don't have either an apology or a resignation for you."

"I thought I made myself pretty clear on Friday about what you needed to give me today, Kendall."

"You did. But I can't authentically give you either of those things right now. What I can give you is my assurance that I've learned from this experience. I think Jill is right. I need to have a better plan for genuinely allowing teens to opt out of games. I also need to be more selective in the games that we play at The Lighthouse. Games should be fun. I want them to help break teens out of their comfort zones. But I also want them to be safe—both physically and emotionally."

Nate paused, seemingly a little disarmed by Kendall's willingness to share what she'd learned.

"I'm really glad to hear that, Kendall," said Nate, with a much softer tone than he'd been using to that point. "If that's the case, though, can't you just say that in a letter of apology like I asked you to?"

Kendall debated internally for a moment, afraid that if she didn't say what she was actually thinking, she never would. She summoned her courage.

"I could, but I won't," she said. "I don't think your request is fair. You deliberately sideswiped me on Friday by not telling me that Jill would be here. That betrayed my trust, Nate. Believe it or not, I've always wanted to learn from you. But I can't do that when you're busy shaming me in front of a parent. I need you to have my back."

Much to Kendall's surprise, Nate said nothing, a rarity for her extremely extroverted boss.

The silence lasted so long that even Kendall—an introvert through and through—began to feel uncomfortable.

"Did you hear me?" Kendall tentatively asked Nate.

"I did," replied Nate. "I think you might be right. When Jill called last week, she backed me into a corner. I felt like I had no choice but to appease her. But that was wrong of me. As your boss and the leader of this congregation, I should have your back. I'm sorry I didn't."

Kendall felt her body relax, although she worried the moment would be short-lived and Nate would soon say something to put her back on the defensive. Instead, he continued. "I appreciate what you said about learning from this experience. It takes a true leader to learn from someone who's pretty hostile toward you. I honestly commend you for finding the grain of truth in what we said last week. For now, that's good enough for me. I don't need a written apology and I certainly don't want your resignation."

Kendall exhaled, stunned by Nate's words. In the years she'd worked for him, never once had he come close to apologizing to her.

Seeing her shock, Nate grinned. "Do me a favor, though, okay? Give me a heads up the next time you decide to upset one of our congregation's key givers."

Kendall sat motionless, trying to process everything Nate had just said. *This* was the boss she wanted to work for all the time. She wondered how she could draw this side out of him more often.

"What?" Nate said, half-jokingly. "Cat got your tongue?"

"Maybe," smiled Kendall, tentative. She got up and left, eager to get out of Nate's office before his evil twin reemerged.

She practically ran to her office, eager to call Frank and fill him in.

"Still want to search for another job?" Frank asked once he was caught up.

"I think so," responded Kendall, less sure of this than she was that morning. "I want to be able to choose to stay or leave, like Jake said. Now it just feels like things aren't quite as urgent as they were last week."

"That's good," answered Frank. "It's better to make a change because you want to than because you have to."

"You can say that again!"

"Okay," joked Frank. "It's better to make a change because you want to than because you have to."

"That was so cheesy," groaned Kendall.

"But you're smiling, aren't you?" asked Frank.

"Indeed," said Kendall, feeling her smile creep into her voice. "And Frank? Thanks, babe."

"For what?"

"For supporting me as I look for other jobs, even though you're not eager to make this change."

"You're welcome," replied Frank. "I might not be eager to make this change, but I am excited for you to see what's out there."

"Me too," agreed Kendall. "See you in a bit."

■ ■ ■

TUESDAY, APRIL 7: AN INTERESTING E-MAIL...OR TWO

Kendall turned her Bible to Exodus, eager to continue journeying with the Israelites. She cracked open her breakfast Pepsi and looked out the sunroom window just in time to see a beautiful sunrise.

"Your mercies are indeed new every morning," she thought to herself before digging into Exodus 4. Today, she felt drawn to Exodus 4:14 and the way in which God provided Moses with exactly the right partner—Aaron—to accomplish his mission to free the Israelites.

She wondered if this was the kind of partnership Jake had been referring to on Saturday when he'd talked about her being released into an environment where she could really flourish. As she read, she sensed that Aaron brought out the best in Moses and that Moses did the same for Aaron.

It was clear to Kendall that this was not the case for her and Nate. She wondered what her ministry might look like if it were.

She sketched out some notes in her journal before reluctantly deciding she better scan her e-mail before it got any later. From the comfort of her prayer chair, Kendall fired up her laptop and logged into her personal Gmail account.

She scrolled through her new e-mails before one caught her eye. "Meet?" it said simply. The sender, Aaron, wasn't one she recognized. She tentatively opened it, ready to click **TRASH** if it ended up being spam.

It wasn't.

Instead, it was a personal message from the senior pastor at one of the churches she'd sent her resume on Saturday. Aaron said he was impressed with her resume and wondered if she'd be open to grabbing a cup of coffee in the next couple of weeks.

Kendall Googled the church, Trinity, and briefly scanned their website. She also clicked on Aaron's picture and was surprised to find someone who looked like he could be her peer. Kendall laughed aloud at Aaron's description and noted that like Jake, he seemed a little obsessed with skinny jeans. She also noted what could only be classified as youth ministry language permeating his bio and description of their church, something she found interesting but curious.

Without hesitation, she flipped open her calendar, checked her availability, and replied to Aaron with a couple of options for getting together.

She then continued sifting through her inbox. She found another e-mail, this one from Bob, with a similar heading: "Interview?"

She opened it and found a similarly worded e-mail from Bob, the head of the search committee at First Church, the church she'd been most excited about on Saturday, largely because it had a female senior pastor.

Without a moment's hesitation, she responded to Bob with the same set of dates she'd just sent Aaron.

By the time Kendall left for work, she'd heard back from both Aaron and Bob, each confirming a meeting two weeks later.

Kendall walked to work, an extra spring in her step.

That morning, she sat in her program planning meeting as Nate droned on about some plans for their big summer kickoff a few weeks later. Not for the first time, she wondered why Nate couldn't be a fraction as compelling with their staff as he was with their congregation.

Since Nate's plans failed to include any mention of the youth, Kendall asked what he was thinking their participation in the summer kickoff would be. "I assumed they'd babysit the kiddos so that parents can actually enjoy their time here," Nate said. "Then, I thought they could clean up, since you're always looking for opportunities for them to serve, Kendall."

Kendall tried hard not to roll her eyes while she debated whether or not to fight this battle. In the end, she decided it was important enough to say something, to try yet again to correct Nate's understanding of both service and intergenerational ministry.

"Actually," said Kendall, "that's not exactly what I had in mind when I said I wanted our teens to serve. It's also not exactly what I had in mind when I asked you what you imagined their participation would look like. I was thinking that we could do a beer and hymn sing under the tent as part of our summer kickoff but rather than have alcohol, we could have root beer kegs. I think our teens and their families would get a big kick out of that. That would also give our teens a chance to really interact with and be part of our congregation. Maybe they'll even be able to connect with some of our older parishioners. If we play our cards right, this could truly be an intergenerational event—"

Nate cut her off. "It *will* be an intergenerational event, Kendall. That's why we're providing babysitters so that families can bring the *whole* family to summer kickoff. You'll let us know who can be there to serve, then?"

Recognizing that nothing she said would change Nate's mind, Kendall swallowed her pride and offered a weak, "Yep. I will."

For the rest of their meeting, she found herself wondering what intergenerational ministry might look like at Trinity and First Church. Both used intergenerational language on their website…but then again, so did Grace. Kendall began daydreaming about Aaron and Jo—the senior pastors at Trinity and First Church. Would they have brushed off her suggestion as Nate had? Or would they have actually been receptive to her ideas? What would it look like for her to truly be able to partner with a church's senior pastor, in much the same way that Moses and Aaron partnered with one another, with gifts that complemented each other's?

For the first time since beginning at Grace, Kendall found herself honestly wondering if her ministry was drawing to a close. It was a strange and hopeful sensation.

■ ■ ■

SATURDAY, APRIL 11: ANOTHER PIECE OF ADVICE

When Kendall arrived at The Perk on Saturday morning, she grabbed her and Jake's usual booth before ordering her grande caramel macchiato. By the time her drink came, Jake had arrived.

She quickly caught him up: About what a great day of ministry she'd had on Sunday, about her surprising conversation with Nate on Monday, and about the e-mails from Aaron and Bob on Tuesday.

As Kendall talked, Nate couldn't hold back his smile. "Sounds like it's been a pretty good week for you, Kendall!"

"A good week? It's been such a confusing week! How do I continue to do good ministry at Grace even while I'm seriously looking for another job? I feel like I'm dancing the Hokey Pokey. I've got one foot in and the other out."

"That's only going to get worse, Kendall. The further you get into this job search, the more you'll feel that tension. You're living in something of a liminal space. It's an in-between, an already, not-yet-there time period."

Although Kendall hated the use of Jake's Christianese, she had to agree that tension was exactly what she'd been feeling the last couple of days as she tried to shepherd her ministry at Grace forward while staying attentive to her own feelings about the prospect of leaving.

"I think you'll find this time to be unusually sacred," continued Jake. "You're going to savor this time with your youth group kids even more than you normally would because you're acutely aware that this might be your last season with them. That will make you grateful for things you wouldn't have previously noticed. You'll also find it easier to let go of some of the conflicts you might have previously run toward. Why fight a battle if you won't be there to see it through?"

"I take it that's spoken from experience?"

"You know it is," replied Jake honestly. "There's been no sweeter times in my ministries than during periods of discernment. I'm not sure why God works that way, but it's been my experience that God does. And that's another thing. I'm convinced God will show up in some unexpected ways during this time. In fact, I've been thinking about that a lot this week. I've been drawn to Exodus lately."

"You're kidding, right, Jake?" Kendall tried to remember whether she'd told Jake this was what she was currently exploring during her quiet times. She told Jake a little bit about her own musings from the last several weeks.

"See," said Jake. "God is already showing up in some unexpected ways. Can I get an Amen?"

"Amen," laughed Kendall.

"Since you've been studying Exodus, you'll appreciate this all the more," Jake continued. "Remember how God provided the Israelites with manna throughout their forty years in the wilderness?"

Kendall nodded, curious where Jake was going with this.

"God told the Israelites to take only the amount of manna that they needed for that day," said Jake. "If they took more, the manna went bad."

"That's nice, Jake," retorted Kendall. "But last time I checked, God wasn't raining manna down on my lawn."

"Of course not. But God is providing for you, just as God provided for the Israelites. This time of discernment will be hard for you, but God will give you what you need, each and every day. God will provide, just as God always provides for God's people."

"What exactly do you think God's providing for me right now?"

"Well, that's largely for you to figure out," replied Jake. "But for starters, it sounds like God's providing you with the opportunity to explore your call and possibly to choose to begin serving in a new ministry."

"I can't even tell you how much I've been thinking about that this last week," said Kendall. "I don't even have another job offer yet and yet it feels so freeing to think that I might actually have a choice to make. Even the possibility of a choice is liberating."

It felt so liberating, in fact, that Frank had even commented on Kendall's "lightness" throughout the week. She'd done her normal complaining about Nate, especially in regard to the summer kickoff. But she'd done it in a less serious, more joking way. Frank told her later how surprised he was that she wasn't more bothered by Nate's denseness. She wholeheartedly attributed her changed perspective to the possibility of having a choice to stay or to go—and even, possibly, to choose between going multiple places. These new possibilities were bringing her a deep sense of hope.

Jake could see that on her face. "Kendall, I believe you're going to have a decision to make in the next few weeks. How will you choose what to do next? To return to our phrase from last week, if two churches call you *and* you're currently serving at another, how will you know where you're actually being called? How will you decide which church to choose? How will you know where you'll fit best?

Immediately, Kendall thought about Nate's sermon last week. She recapped it for Jake. "Based on our conversation last time, I wonder if God really cares. I mean, is God's call to me specific to *one* church or is it just for me to do youth ministry somewhere?"

Kendall paused. "But now that I ask that, it feels heretical. Is it?"

"I don't think so," replied Jake slowly, like the sage Kendall thought he was. "In fact, I think one of the biggest fallacies of evangelicalism is this idea that God has *one* path for you and it's up to you to find it. How did we even begin to think that's the way it works?"

Kendall shook her head in disbelief. "I don't know, but we certainly have."

"I don't think God gives a rip about what we decide," said Jake, unafraid of offending Kendall.

"You're going to have to explain that one to me," replied Kendall honestly.

"Scripture is filled with so many big picture things. Most Christians would agree that if you're loving God, loving others, doing justice, and walking humbly, you're doing God's will. Does that seem fair?"

"I think so," replied Kendall, still unsure what Jake was getting at.

"If that's the case, then as long as you're doing those things, I don't really think God cares which church you work for. So, if you get an offer from both churches and are therefore called by both, I think it's entirely possible for you to choose either and still please God."

Kendall considered this for a moment before replying. "That's pretty liberating too!"

"It is," agreed Jake. "But it also means that you *really* might have a choice here. That if you get an offer from both churches, then where you go is, in fact, actually up to you. How will you choose?"

"I don't know! If it doesn't matter, then maybe I should just flip a coin!"

"It would certainly be easier," agreed Jake. "But I don't think that's the best use of the decision-making capabilities that God's given you."

"Agreed." Kendall sighed. "But the whole church hiring process is like the most awkward dating relationship in the history of the world. It's long…it's slow…people are so intent on putting their best foot forward that sometimes you don't even really get a realistic sense of what you're signing up for. I mean, when I said *yes* to Grace, I was ecstatic. After that disaster that was my first job, all fourteen months of it—and the near disaster that followed at my second job, I thought I did much better screening Grace for fit. We dated longer. Nate met Frank, but didn't interview him. I met the kids involved in the youth group. We talked about philosophy of ministry. We were aligned on ALL THE THINGS. I even liked Nate when we met—he was dynamic and fun, like he is in the pulpit and with our congregation. I honestly thought I'd love working for him, but clearly, I was wrong. If I got it wrong here, then how do I know I won't get it wrong again?"

"You don't, Kendall. If you decide to leave Grace, there's a distinct possibility that you *will* get it wrong again. But there's also the distinct possibility that you'll get it *right*, that you'll end up in a place that really is a good fit for you. My hunch is that every time you make a transition, you'll learn more about what you're looking for. You'll get better and better at dating churches and finding out what a church—and its leadership—is really like. You're going to be able to see past their veneer in a way that you haven't always been able to."

"But how? How do I do that?"

"Well, that comes back to fit. Remember, you're interviewing these churches as much as they're interviewing you. Based on your experience so far, what's important to you about the next church you work at?"

"That's easy," said Kendall. "I want to be part of a staff that functions as a team. I want my senior pastor to have my back and to support me. That doesn't mean they can't criticize me or give me constructive feedback. I want them to be able to challenge me. But I want to be able to challenge them, too. I want to collaborate with my staff in a genuine partnership that benefits the entire church. And that's another thing. I want to work in a place that truly values intergenerational ministry. That's such a buzzword right now that I feel like everybody *says* they're intergenerational, but not a lot of places really are. I want my next church *not* to program as though teens are better off when they're seen but not heard."

"That's a pretty good list, Kendall."

"I worry that it's too good."

"What do you mean?"

"Well," said Kendall, "does such a place even exist?"

"It does," assured Jake. "Don't let your less-than-stellar experience at Grace convince you otherwise. There are good churches that would relish having a youth pastor like you. You just have to find each other. That's what fit is really about. It's asking if you agree about the important things in ministry—those things you just rattled off. Are you aligned in your ministry philosophies? In your values? Could you see yourself serving at a particular place, with a particular group of people? That's fit, too. Good hiring processes are designed to flesh that out for you; they're designed to show you whether or not you fit in a particular church culture."

"I think I really underestimated the role that church culture plays in all of this," reflected Kendall. "I thought all churches had the same culture, but I'm learning they don't."

"That's for sure. Another element of fit is thinking through your gifts alongside a church's needs. If your gifts match a church's actual needs, that can indicate you might be a good fit there."

Kendall considered what Jake had said. "That's an interesting way of thinking about it."

Jake checked the time on his cell phone and apologetically got up. "Should we meet again in two weeks, after your first round of interviews is finished?"

"Yes, please!" responded Kendall excitedly. "But if I feel like I'm going to jump off the cliff before then, I'm gonna call you. Is that still okay?"

"You know it is," Jake said. "But in that case, I'll be praying that I don't hear from you during these next two weeks."

"Perfect," laughed Kendall, as she hugged her mentor, once again thankful for his years of wisdom.

■ ■ ■

MONDAY, APRIL 20: THE FIRST INTERVIEW

The next two weeks passed uneventfully, which Kendall was thankful for.

During that time, she heard from the other three churches she'd sent her resume to. One said they would not hire a woman as their lead youth pastor but wondered if she'd be interested in an office administrator role. Rather than be offended, Kendall laughed and tried to figure out how she'd missed the fact that this church was complementarian. Normally, she could pick them out a mile away, either from their website language or pictures of their all-male staff.

The other two churches replied thoughtfully and personally. They complimented Kendall on her experience but informed her they'd already filled the roles she'd applied for. Relieved to know where she stood, Kendall began focusing on First Church and Trinity. As her interviews approached, she got increasingly excited.

As Jake had predicted, she wasn't as troubled as she thought she'd be by having one foot in and one foot out of her ministry at Grace. Instead, she'd gained perspective from this liminal space, an acute awareness of God's activity in every realm of her life.

While things had calmed down with Nate over the last two weeks, nothing had really changed. This awareness made Kendall feel content, like she was truly resting in God's will. She was shepherding her teens well, while at the same time actively pushing on some doors to see which, if any, God opened for her. She sensed that she was doing her part in her unfolding story while trusting God to do God's part.

Despite her overall contentment, now that the day of her first interview was here, Kendall was struggling. Her emotions were running unchecked, but she'd been so busy all day that she'd scarcely had a moment to register them, let alone process what she was feeling.

She'd prepped for The Lighthouse's Wednesday night gathering and their Mexico mission trip meeting. She'd had a dinner meeting with one of her adult leaders who was struggling in her marriage. She'd successfully avoided Nate all day.

Before she knew it, it was time to drive to First Church for her interview with their search committee.

From the car she called Frank, who picked up on the first ring.

"Tell me something good," said Kendall as soon as he answered.

"What?!" joked Frank. "No hello or anything?"

"You know I love you but I don't time for that. I'm freaking out here!"

"We both knew you would be, Kendall. Relax. You've got this."

"How do you know I've got this?"

"Because you're you! First Church would be a fool not to hire you. If First Church is the right place for you, God will open the door. Then your only job is to move through it."

"But what if I blow it?"

"You won't!" assured Frank. "But if you do, then it wasn't meant to be. Then God's got another plan for you. Trust that. You do your part and let God do God's part."

"I've been thinking about that all day," admitted Kendall.

"Rest in that, okay? And call me afterward."

"Will do," said Kendall as she hung up. She used the rest of the drive to pray that she wouldn't blow the interview or look like an idiot. She recognized her prayer was a little self-centered, but it was honestly where she was.

After about forty minutes of driving, Kendall got to First Church. She drove around the building twice to scope it out, then drove around the neighborhood to scout it out a little bit as well, finally pulling into the parking lot at a neighboring CVS. She checked her teeth to make sure no dinner remained, then reapplied her lipstick. It was time. She drove the block back to First Church, where a woman waited outside the door—to greet her, she hoped. Kendall recognized her as the senior pastor and was thrilled to get the chance to meet her. She wondered if she'd be in her interview.

Kendall checked her appearance once more in the rearview mirror, grabbed her purse, and got out of the car. As she did, the woman made her way down the steps toward her and extended her hand. "I'm Jo," she said enthusiastically. "I'm the senior pastor here at First Church. You must be Kendall. It's so nice to meet you."

Kendall smiled. Jo was warm and personable. She liked her immediately. "It's good to be here."

Jo led Kendall into the building, talking as they walked. "Our search committee is very excited to meet you. You wrote quite a compelling cover letter. Your approach to dealing with teens' questions really intrigued and resonated with them. I won't be in your meeting with the search committee, but I'm hoping we can chat after it's over, if you've got any energy left at that point. I know how exhausting these kinds of interviews are."

Kendall nodded and Jo smiled. She motioned to a room with double doors painted in a myriad of colors. Kendall assumed this was their youth room and that someone had simply let the youth paint it however they wanted. As if she knew what Kendall was thinking, Jo announced, "We thought we'd do the interview in our youth room. Several years ago, our youth decorated it themselves!"

Although Jo smiled proudly, Kendall wasn't so sure this was something to be proud of. Just once she'd like to walk into a youth room that had been professionally decorated and designed to give teens the most welcoming atmosphere possible.

Kendall took stock off the room. As was typical of every youth room she'd ever been in, the center was filled with mismatched couches, clearly acquired one at a time as people lovingly offered their reject furniture to a church who always said "Yes!" to whatever anyone was giving away. On one side of the couches was a coffee bar area. On the other, there was a large ping-pong table. A small stage was set up at the front of the room.

Once Kendall got to the center of the room, Jo introduced her to Bob, the head of the search committee and the person she'd previously e-mailed with, and then made a graceful exit, assuring her she'd be back at the end of the interview.

Bob introduced Kendall to everyone in the room. There was Hank, the chair of the elder board; Sarah, a parent and longtime volunteer; Matilda, the mother of a junior high student; Ted, the father of a third grader; Mike, a high school senior; and Amy, a high school freshman. Bob was a bit older than Kendall had imagined him to be. As she peered around the room, she couldn't help but think the committee felt a little predictable—as though every group within the church was represented by exactly one person on the committee.

Kendall pushed that thought from her mind and focused. For the next ninety minutes, the search committee grilled Kendall in what felt like a carefully choreographed routine. Each person had a list of questions in front of them and had clearly been assigned one or two to ask. As far as Kendall could tell, there was no deviating from the script.

By the end of their time together, she'd been asked about her faith journey and when she came to know Jesus; how she'd structure a weekly youth gathering; her strategies for transitioning the junior high students to the high school ministry; how she'd deal with a difficult parent; ideas for what to discuss with the teens; her approach to Scripture; and her stance on LGBTQ issues, race issues, and refugees.

Kendall felt good about her answers. She wasn't asked about anything she hadn't already considered at length. Nothing made her stumble, which made her feel confident—not overly rehearsed or practiced, but honest. At the same time, not a single question made her think deeply. Nothing made her really begin dreaming about or getting excited about the prospect of ministry at First Church.

At the conclusion of the interview, Bob asked, "Do you have any questions for us, Kendall?"

She did. Since her meeting with Jake, she'd been thinking nonstop about what she wanted to know about First Church and Trinity. She hoped to ask questions to learn more about the church but also to help her discern whether or not she'd be a good fit there.

She looked at Mike. "I think it's awesome that you're here, Mike. As a senior, I'm curious. What have been the most significant parts of your faith journey here at First Church? What's really formed your faith?"

Without pausing to think for even a second, Mike answered. "Oh you know, just hanging out with my friends. It's so good to have a place to come where I can be around other people who believe in God and stuff."

Kendall smiled encouragingly, hoping that Mike would continue. When he didn't, she prompted for more. "I love that, Mike. But what would you say has been significant about those relationships for you? How have they helped you grow in your relationship with Jesus?"

Like a deer caught in the headlights, Mike looked around helplessly. He finally motioned to Amy and said, "That sounds like a great question for Amy to answer. Amy, what do you think?"

Amy also looked like a deer caught in the headlights. Only she had no other, younger teen to stick with the question. Reluctantly, Amy said, "I just think like there's something so like powerful about being together with my friends worshiping. When we're all singing one of our favorite worship songs, that's just like so awesome."

Although Kendall could see that the poor girl was trying, she felt like her answer was a bit lackluster. She suspected that her own teens at Grace would answer the question very differently, that they'd share stories about times during their discussions when one of their friends said something that made them think about Scripture in an entirely new way. They might even talk about a time when one of their friends directly challenged something they said.

Mike's and Amy's inability to answer basic questions made Kendall wonder about their current youth gatherings. She turned to Sarah, the longtime volunteer. "Tell me about your Wednesday night gatherings. What are they like?"

Sarah described a pretty vanilla youth ministry comprised of hangout time, worship, a talk, and occasional small groups.

"How does your youth ministry go about welcoming students from the fringes into your midst?" Kendall asked Sarah, curious.

"We're a judgment-free zone," Sarah quickly responded. "Teens know they're welcome here."

"Judgment-free" was a trigger phrase for Kendall, who knew that teens were inherently judgmental. This was even true developmentally for teens, as they transitioned from concrete thinking, where they used judgments to categorize people and things, to more abstract thought. With this in mind, Kendall probed further. "Let's say a junior walks in who's been on your roster forever but has never actually attended youth ministry. How would you welcome her?"

Again, Sarah responded quickly. "We're really careful not to over-program our youth gatherings. We know that teens have been in school all day. By the time they get here, they need a little less structure."

Kendall heard that coded Christianese for what it was: An admission that they currently had no plan for welcoming teens into their youth ministry.

Kendall filed that away as disappointing, but not surprising. She didn't know of a lot of ministries who actually had such a plan. Plus, leadership and hospitality—the two things required to enact it—were two of her gifts. Clearly, those traits were needed here. She wondered if maybe this was what Jake was talking about when he said that her gifts should be aligned with a church's needs.

More important to her than that, though, was knowing how the teens at First Church were being discipled. She turned to Hank, the chair of the elder board. "As an elder at First Church, what's most important to you about your youth ministry here? What would success look like for your next youth pastor?"

"Numbers," Hank boomed. "We are a rapidly-growing church committed to reaching out to our community. We want to see our numbers grow. A successful youth pastor will be one who doubles our current attendance in two years."

"What is your current youth group attendance?" questioned Kendall.

Now it was Hank's turn to look around helplessly, clearly unsure how to answer. This seemed like a big red flag. Sarah jumped in. "We've got around twenty teens who come right now."

"And how many people worship with your congregation during the course of a weekend?"

Hank was all over that answer. "About 400," he said quickly.

Kendall did the math. A healthy youth ministry was typically about ten percent of the worshiping population of a church. So, by that metric, their youth ministry had room to grow. She wondered why their numbers were low. She tucked that information away, hoping to return to it later.

But she didn't want to lose this train of thought, especially since Hank had such a strong reaction to the numbers game. Kendall asked another question. "What kinds of things would you hope a youth pastor would do to grow your ministry?"

Mike looked around before answering for the team. "Well, at my friend's church, they're always hosting concerts and fifth quarter events. I'd really like it if we could do some more social events. I mean that's really what we want. We're busy. We just want to come here and have fun."

Inwardly, Kendall cringed. Mike's words made her think this was not the kind of ministry she wanted to lead. It was also not the kind of ministry she was good at leading.

Just as she was about to write off First Church, Ted spoke. Up to this point, he had been silent, with the exception of the interview question he'd been assigned. "I know that my kids are little, but I've got to tell you: There are plenty of places where they can go to have fun," he shared, a little awkwardly. "And there are plenty of places teens can go to have fun. What I don't think they can get other places is Jesus. I'm hopeful that our next youth pastor will really take an interest in discipling our young people. I hope she will really try to develop healthy followers of Jesus."

Ah, Kendall thought. Finally, someone was speaking her love language.

"What do you think a healthy follower of Jesus looks like?" Kendall asked, hoping Ted would answer on behalf of the search committee.

Instead, Hank interjected. "That sounds like a question we should have asked you! How would you answer that, Kendall?"

Kendall thought for a second. She knew her answer. She'd spent a lot of time thinking about this very question. But she really wanted to hear how this committee would respond to it. She knew instinctively that this was how she'd figure out if she was a good fit here. She countered diplomatically. "Hank, I'd love to answer your question. I'd be happy to. But I'd really like to hear *your* answer first. Would you be willing to share before I do?"

Hank looked a little perturbed, leaving Kendall feeling as though this was the moment she'd blown her interview. As she tried to silence her inner monologue, Matilda, who'd also asked nothing but her assigned question, interrupted. "I'd be happy to, Kendall. I think a healthy follower of Jesus prioritizes their faith, something we know because they're always at church. A healthy follower of Jesus loves others and tolerates people, even those who are different from them."

Kendall waited a beat, interested to see if anyone would add anything more to Matilda's response. When no one did, she replied. "Thanks, Matilda. I also think that a healthy follower of Jesus prioritizes their faith and loves others. I wonder, though, about your use of the word *tolerate*."

Kendall paused, trying to figure out how to phrase her concern in a way that wouldn't offend Matilda or anyone else. Just as she figured it out, Hank interrupted. "I think we can all agree that we want our teens to be healthy followers of Jesus. That's good enough, don't you think?"

As if by magic, Jo appeared back in the room, indicating it was time for this part of the interview to conclude. Kendall shook everyone's hand before turning to Jo, who ushered her through the colorful doors.

"How are you doing, dear?" Jo asked, genuinely concerned.

"Well," said Kendall, "I could sure use something to drink."

"Let's walk over to Pete's Coffee and we can get to know one another a bit more. Does that sound okay?"

Kendall nodded.

They chatted as they walked; Jo was good at making small talk in a way that put Kendall at ease. By the time they reached Pete's, they had struck up a friendly banter.

They sat down at a table. "How was that process for you?" Jo asked.

"Exhausting," replied Kendall honestly.

"I know," laughed Jo. "Hank can be a bit much, can't he?"

That comment helped Kendall relax and gave her permission to speak honestly. She figured she had nothing to lose. As Frank had told her, either God was going to open this door or God wasn't.

"He really can be," Kendall began. "He caught me off guard a couple of times. I know I've only known you both for about five seconds, but you seem very different. I'm curious how you lead with him as your elder board chair."

"You're perceptive," replied Jo. "We are very different. I was hesitant about that initially. But in our congregation, once the board is elected, they elect a chair. Hank wasn't my choice, but he was the board's choice and I have to respect that. Much to my surprise, I've actually led better with him than I've led with other board chairs, I think in part *because* of our differences."

Kendall found much of what Jo said intriguing. It connected with what she and Jake had been discussing about fit. She was also curious about Hank's election as board chair. Her experience thus far had been that pastors either assigned that role to the person they most got along with on the board, or they seeded the election so that their choice for that role was the only person running for it. The idea that Hank was chair even though he wasn't Jo's choice said something about her leadership, although she was still trying to figure out what.

Jo interrupted her thoughts. "Your resume is impressive, Kendall. I'd like to know why you're considering making a move."

Kendall had been bracing for this question all night. She began, tentatively. "I've been in my current position for three full years. It's been good in many ways. God has shown up. My ministry has borne fruit. And I've learned a lot about who I am as a youth pastor."

"And yet?" encouraged Jo.

Kendall debated with herself a moment before deciding to simply share her truth. "And yet I'm having some trouble with my boss. We don't have any real synergy. I'm starting to wonder if it would be better for both of us—and maybe even for my church—if we parted ways."

Jo nodded. "I'm curious, then. You mentioned not having any synergy with your boss. That's obviously important to you. What do you think that synergy would look like?"

Kendall nearly burst into tears. Until this moment, she hadn't realized just how meaningful a question this was for her.

"I think synergy looks like genuine partnership. Like someone who makes me better and who I make better, too. It means trust. It means my boss has my back, even during those moments when I get it wrong, which will happen because I'm still learning how to do ministry effectively. Plus, I like to experiment with new ways of doing things and that also means that sometimes I'm going to get it wrong. Synergy also looks like challenging me to get better at my craft. It means giving me chances to take risks, even if I fail miserably."

Jo smiled. "That's a great, thoughtful answer, Kendall. I'm sure you have some questions for me as well. What would you like to know?"

Kendall mentally cycled through the dozen or so questions she'd prepared. "What value does your youth ministry bring your congregation?"

"What a great question!" Jo said earnestly. "A youth ministry adds tremendous value to our congregation. I'm sure you heard from Hank how much he wants our next youth pastor to numerically grow our youth ministry. As a senior pastor, I can attest to the fact that a lot of my peers look at having the right youth minister as a key to their financial and numerical success. They'll tell you that the right youth pastor can bring in more than enough families to cover the cost of their salary and then some. There's some truth to that. But that's not the value the youth ministry brings to our congregation."

"What is that value?" asked Kendall, feeling hopeful.

"The value our youth ministry brings to our congregation is the youth themselves. The youth challenge our adults—to be better followers of Jesus, to think differently, and to actively work to bring God's kingdom to the world. The youth help our adults grow in their faith in the same way we want our adults to help our teens grow in their faith. We believe in mutuality and the idea that every member of our community has something to contribute to it. Our youth are no different. They aren't somehow partial, or inferior, members of First Church. They're full members who bring the same value to our church as our adults."

Kendall nodded, silently affirming Jo's answer. She thought about Nate's plan to utilize Grace's teens as babysitters and janitors at their summer kickoff and wondered what Jo would say about such a thing.

"I know we could keep chatting, but I'm also aware of the time," Jo said. "It's getting late. Can we keep processing individually and then check back in with one another later this week to see where we are?"

"That sounds great," agreed Kendall.

She and Jo walked back to First Church, where they shook hands at her car door. Kendall climbed in, exhausted. As soon as Jo disappeared back into the church building, she called Frank.

"Well?" he asked as soon as he picked up. "How'd it go?"

"It was good…I think."

"I feel like your words aren't matching your tone. What do you mean?"

"I'm not sure," said Kendall. "There was a lot that was good. This senior pastor for one. I really liked her, Frank."

"I'm not surprised," replied Frank. "I thought working for a female would be a plus for you. It excites me, too. I've never attended a church with a female senior pastor!"

"I know," said Kendall excitedly. "I think she'd be good for us in so many ways. Tonight she shepherded me to and from my interview with the search committee and then we talked for about an hour afterward. She's super personal. I felt like our conversation was very honest. I think I'd really like working with and for her."

"But?"

"But…there was the committee. I just don't know what to make of them."

"What do you mean?"

"Well, they seemed so rehearsed. They literally went around in a circle each asking me one specific question off a list. It all felt a little disingenuous. But here's the strangest part. I asked them some pretty basic questions about their youth ministry and they had a really hard time answering them."

Frank laughed. "We both know there's nothing basic about your questions, Kendall. That's one of the things the kids at Grace love about you. You make them think."

"You might be right," agreed Kendall. "But still. I asked them what a healthy follower of Jesus looks like and it felt like no one could tell me. When one person finally gave a semi-decent answer, I pushed back and Hank—the head of their elder board— literally interrupted me and said that we could all agree on the fact that we want to cultivate healthy followers of Jesus."

"You can, can't you?" asked Frank.

"Sure…well, no, actually. Because I'm not sure what they were describing would produce healthy followers of Jesus, *and* more importantly, I'm not sure we'd agree on what a healthy follower of Jesus actually looks like."

"Oh." Frank exhaled. "You're right. That's a little weird. So, do you not want to move on with this church?"

Kendall paused a beat.

"No," she replied. "I don't think that's it either. I'm curious about this church. Jo, the senior pastor, and I agreed we'd both continue to process and then we'd reconnect at the end of the week to see where we are."

"And where are you right now?" asked Frank.

"The corner of 63rd and Main," replied Kendall with a smile.

"You know that's not what I meant," retorted Frank.

"I know." Kendall sighed. "There's a chance that I'm trying to avoid your question because honestly, Frank, I don't know. I like Jo. A lot. But if this search committee is an honest reflection of their congregation, I'm not sure I'd want to work there."

"Is Nate better than the search committee?"

"In a way, I think he might be," replied Kendall honestly. "Actually,

I don't know that it's a matter of him being better or worse. I think it comes back to what Jake and I were talking about a couple of weeks ago. I don't want to leave just to leave. I want to run toward something better, not just flee from something bad. Based on tonight, I'm not sure this would be better. Although I like Jo. Have I mentioned that?"

"Once or twice," said Frank. Kendall could hear his grin through the phone. "What do you need when you get home tonight?"

"Nachos, a margarita, and a shoulder rub?"

"You got it," said Frank lovingly.

When Kendall pulled up, Frank was waiting for her with all three things. Kendall sat down, exhausted by the day but grateful for every part of it.

"You know," she told Frank before they'd even gotten into the house, "I'm not sure First Church is the right fit for me. But I am sure of this: I need to be interviewing right now. Jake is right. This process is so helpful. The idea of choice is still empowering, but what I saw tonight is that even the interviews themselves are helpful. They're clarifying what I think is important to ministry."

"I can see that in your posture and confidence," agreed Frank. "You're doing better at Grace than you have in a long time. I'm proud of you, Kendall."

"Thanks, babe."

And with that, Kendall and Frank collapsed onto the couch, eager to watch the next episode of their current binge watch—*Parks and Recreation*—and finish off their pitcher of margaritas.

■ ■ ■

THURSDAY, APRIL 23: ANOTHER FIRST INTERVIEW

Tuesday and Wednesday, Kendall focused exclusively on her ministry at Grace. She was grateful she had no interviews on those days, especially during this busy season. She felt relieved to have meaningful work to do at Grace, even as she discerned whether a new role might be in her future. Just as Jake had predicted, she was acutely aware of how God was at work in her teens and leaders. Because of the surprising sweetness of this season, she found herself grieving the mere thought of leaving Grace even though she had no job offers in hand. For three years, this had been her church home and she and Frank had devoted themselves to it.

After a frantic morning at Grace, Kendall took Thursday afternoon off in order to spend some time with God before her interview at Trinity. Once again, she dove into the book of Exodus. Today, she read Exodus 5. As she thought about the Israelites being forced to make bricks without straw, she couldn't help but think about her situation at Grace.

She flashed back to Nate's request for her to approve her games and lesson plans with him. Although she'd talked her way out of it, she felt as though this was the equivalent of making bricks without straw. She worried if she stayed at Grace she'd always be expected to minister in suboptimal conditions. She had a difficult time imagining a situation in which that might change. She feared it wouldn't unless she could figure out how to become a genuine partner to Nate. But that was the catch. She couldn't do that alone. By definition, partnering required two people.

After her quiet time, Kendall journaled for a while before leaving a note for Frank and heading out the door.

She and Aaron had agreed to meet at the Five Guys two suburbs over. It was far enough away from home that she felt confident no one she knew would see her. This worry reminded Kendall just how much she felt like she was cheating on Grace with Aaron. Once again, she wondered if it was wrong for her to even be taking this meeting.

When she got to Five Guys, Kendall self-consciously looked around the restaurant trying to identify Aaron. Before long, she spotted someone slightly older than her, balding, sitting in the corner booth; he seemed to match the picture she'd seen on Trinity's website. He smiled slightly before getting up, brushing off his skinny jeans, and then extending his hand. "Kendall, I presume?" he asked confidently.

Kendall nodded her head in agreement, smiling as she noticed the hoodie Aaron was wearing. She wondered how he would have reacted had she worn hers. Instead of commenting, she simply said, "You must be Aaron. It's good to meet you."

She and Aaron headed to the counter to order, waited for their burgers and fries, and returned to their table. Kendall noted that she didn't feel the easy banter that she had with Jo. She wondered what that might mean but chose not to dwell on it. Instead, she fought to stay present in her conversation with Aaron.

Over dinner, Aaron shared extensively about the ministry of Trinity. Even though it was evident how much he cared about the congregation and its youth ministry, Kendall found something about Aaron annoying. She started to wonder if he was ever going to get around to actually asking her a question.

Rather than dwell on that, she instead tried to focus on what he was saying. There was something about the way he discussed youth ministry that made her wonder if this was his background. She remembered thinking that when she'd read his bio on the church's website as well. Curious, Kendall asked about the insider's language she heard Aaron using.

He broke out in a broad grin and said, "Once a youth pastor, always a youth pastor, right? It's that obvious, huh?"

"Yeah, it kind of is," Kendall agreed.

"I will say," continued Aaron, "I am a better senior pastor because I began in youth ministry. I have an appreciation for young people. I know they're the church—not just of tomorrow but of today. I care about what teens think and know they have gifts to offer our entire congregation. That's why we work really hard at Trinity to integrate teens into every part of our congregation's life."

"Tell me more about that," said Kendall, intrigued, hoping that perhaps his was a vision for intergenerational ministry that extended beyond lip service.

"In our congregation, Youth Sunday used to be a thing. If you're not familiar with Youth Sunday, it's a day when the youth take over a congregation's worship service. I say take over because that's truly what it felt like. Once a year, the teens would come and lead worship. But they made it clear they were doing it *their* way. It felt like for that one Sunday, they made church exactly what they wanted it to be. The rest of the congregation found that to be isolating. Instead of uniting us, Youth Sunday began to feel really divisive. So, a few years ago, we made it our goal to replace Youth Sunday with regular involvement from the youth in our worship service."

"What does that actually look like?" wondered Kendall aloud.

"We don't discriminate based on age," began Aaron. "If someone has the right gifts to serve, we invite them to serve, regardless of whether they're ten or 100. We've got youth who serve as greeters, operate our tech, and play in the praise band. Occasionally, youth even share reflections and testimonies. As a congregation, we work together to develop the gifts of our teens, in the same way we want to teach adults how to use their gifts to benefit our entire community."

"I love that!" replied Kendall.

"I'm glad to hear it," said Aaron with a smile. "Speaking of gifts, can you tell me a little about yours?"

"I'd love to," said Kendall, encouraged that Aaron had asked her something she'd recently been thinking about so deeply. For the next few minutes, Kendall told Aaron about her gifts of leadership, teaching, and hospitality.

"Funny," Aaron said after listening to Kendall. "Those are my top three gifts as well!"

Kendall smiled, although inwardly she wondered whether or not that was actually a good thing. It was obvious her gifts were needed at First Church. She wondered if they were equally needed here at Trinity or if Aaron's gifts eliminated the need for hers.

The two chatted easily for a few more minutes. Aaron asked Kendall about her dreams for ministry, how she'd integrate teens into the larger church, and what family ministry looked like to her.

After the conversation hit a lull, Aaron started to wrap things up. "I've really enjoyed meeting with you today, Kendall. Can you send me a link to your teaching? I'd like to get a feel for your style and then check back in with you."

"I'd be happy too," said Kendall, sensing that their meeting was coming to a close. Not wanting to lose the opportunity to ask Aaron a question, she decided to ask the same one she'd asked the search committee at First Church. "Before we head out, can you tell me what's most important to you about Trinity's youth ministry? What would success look like for the next youth pastor?"

"I'm so glad you asked," said Aaron with a smile. "It's important to me that our youth ministry is a place where teens can go to authentically explore Scripture and ask questions so that they can learn how to follow Jesus in their everyday lives. Success for our next youth pastor would include the ability to help teens get serious about following Jesus and the ability to integrate them into the life of our congregation."

Kendall nodded her head in agreement, struck by how different Aaron's answer was from the one she'd gotten from the search committee at First Church. "Thanks, Aaron. I really appreciate what you just said."

"Let's chat soon, okay?" asked Aaron. "Send me that link and I'll give you a call after I watch it to let you know about next steps."

"Perfect," said Kendall as she stood up, grabbed her purse, and extended her hand out to Aaron, who shook it with an iron-like grasp.

Together, Aaron and Kendall walked out to their cars, chatting about their plans for the weekend. As they did, Kendall realized that the earlier discomfort she'd felt with Aaron was gone. Their conversation now flowed freely.

As Kendall got into her car, she quietly gave God thanks for the night she'd just had. She could honestly picture herself working for Aaron at Trinity. It was a thought that excited her a lot.

She drove home in silence, alone with her thoughts. She contemplated all she'd learned from Aaron about Trinity and all she'd learned on Monday about First Church. She wondered if one of these two places might be her next church home.

As excited as she was by that prospect, she also felt grieved by the thought of leaving Grace. She struggled to understand what that might mean for her, and if it might suggest God was calling her to stay there after all.

Back at home, Kendall walked in the back door and slipped off her shoes, eager to talk to Frank, who was crashed on the couch, playing Zelda. "How'd it go?" he asked, not yet looking away from the game.

"It was good," Kendall said. "Really good, actually. Which is strange because it didn't start out particularly well. In fact, it was a little awkward. I didn't get a great vibe from Aaron initially."

"Oh?"

"He talked a *lot*," said Kendall, moving in front of the TV and intentionally trying to obstruct Frank's view of Zelda so she could get his full attention.

"Hey!" exclaimed Frank. "What are you doing? You're about to make me lose!"

"I know," replied Kendall, with a grin.

"Really?" pouted Frank as Zelda died. "You couldn't have just waited for me to finish before you recapped everything?"

"Wow!" said Kendall. "This from the guy who didn't want me making any decisions without his input. I thought you'd be eager to hear everything so that you could help decide our future."

As Kendall turned and headed for the door, Frank stood and walked toward her.

"I *am* eager to hear about your interview. But I was in the middle of a game—one that you know I love. Had you just let me finish, I would have been all ears."

"I'm sorry, Frank," muttered Kendall. "Really, I am. I'm just so confused. I don't know what to do."

"How about we start over?" asked Frank, taking Kendall's hand and leading her to the couch. "You said that Aaron talked a lot. I bet I know how that went over with my introverted wife."

Kendall smiled. "You know me too well. All Aaron's talking came off as pretty arrogant even though I don't think he meant it to. I think he just really loves his congregation and was excited to share his passion for ministry with me. When he finally got around to asking questions, he asked good ones. He even asked me about my gifts. It turns out that our gifts are the same: leadership, teaching, and hospitality."

"Well," said Frank, "that sounds awesome! Wouldn't it be fun to work with someone who understands you that well?"

"I know," said Kendall. "Maybe it would. But when I think more about my conversation with Jake I wonder how frustrating it might be to work with someone whose gifts are exactly the same as mine. Does Trinity really need another person like that? It sounds like I might just be duplicating exactly what they've already got."

"That could be," said Frank. "But maybe you wouldn't so much be duplicating Aaron's gifts as bringing those same gifts to the youth ministry. If you ask me, that could make for some great synergy between the two of you! Where'd you leave things?"

"I'm going to send him a link to my teaching. He's going to watch it and then give me a call to decide what happens next."

"Sounds good," said Frank. "So how does it feel to have things moving along so well with not one but two different churches?"

"Honestly, it feels great," said Kendall. "Better than I actually thought it would. I'm already starting to dream about what ministry could look like in both of these places. But that's also making me sad about the prospect of leaving Grace."

"Really?" asked Frank. "After the way Nate's treated you, I thought the only thing you'd feel about the prospect of leaving is happy."

"I know," said Kendall. "But the last couple of weeks have gone so well. Plus, I know you don't actually want to leave our neighborhood. Maybe we should just stay."

"You're right," began Frank. "I still don't really want to leave our neighborhood. But as you told me before, neither of these churches would *require* us to move, though it might be more convenient if we did. Let's just keep seeing how things shape up with them before we put a lot of energy into a decision that's not yet ours to make. As for Grace, I think the good vibes you're feeling there are only temporary. It's like the eye of a storm. With how volatile things have been with Nate lately, things will get bad again. It's just a matter of when."

"I know that." Kendall sighed. "At least most of the time. You know I love talking to you about this, but I'm exhausted. Want to watch some more *Parks and Rec*?"

"Absolutely," replied Frank. "Let me just go grab some food first."

"While you do that, I'm going to do important things like send my teaching link to Aaron."

"I'm doing important things, too!" replied Frank jokingly. Kendall sent a follow-up e-mail to Aaron, sharing how much she'd enjoyed their conversation and how much she looked forward to hearing from him after he reviewed her teaching.

■ ■ ■

FRIDAY, APRIL 24: TWO IMPORTANT DEVELOPMENTS

Although the week had been good, by the time Friday came, Kendall was exhausted and relieved that it was her day off this week. She hoped she could finally get some much-needed rest—both physically and emotionally.

Shortly after grabbing her breakfast Pepsi, the phone rang. Seeing that it was Bob from First Church, she quickly picked up, relieved that she'd thought to enter both Bob and Aaron into her contact info so that she wouldn't let their calls go to voicemail.

"Hi Bob!" she answered.

"Hi Kendall," replied Bob. "We just wanted to thank you so much for coming to interview with us earlier this week."

Kendall felt her heart fall, confident Bob was about to tell her they'd decided to go a different route. Instead, he continued. "We were really impressed with you and would like to move you forward in the process. To do that, we'd like three things from you. First, could you e-mail me a list of references? We'd like one of those references to be from Grace so they can attest to your current work. Secondly, we'd love to see a writing sample. Could you e-mail me one of your lessons? Something that you think is representative of who you are and how you teach? Third, we'd like to set up an interview with you and the board. Could you join us next Wednesday around 4:00 for that? We realize that's your youth group night but we'd like to keep things moving. We're hoping that a 4 p.m. start would allow you to get back in time for your gathering at Grace."

Kendall agreed to all three of those things and thanked Bob for the update. As she hung up the phone, she felt conflicted. She hadn't considered having to give a reference from Grace. Doing so seemed complicated. She wondered how to go about it without prematurely alerting—or even worrying—others that she was thinking about leaving. She wanted to be able to leave on her terms and feared that if word got out she was looking elsewhere, Nate wouldn't hesitate to fire her.

The phone rang again. This time it was Aaron.

She picked up, convinced once again that it would be bad news.

"Hi Kendall," said Aaron. "I just finished watching your teaching sample. I've got to tell you, whenever someone says their gift is teaching, I dread watching them teach. I'm always fearful that what I see won't live up to my expectation. But yours did. In fact, it exceeded it. You really are a gifted teacher. The way you broke down difficult concepts for your teens and engaged them in conversation throughout your talk was truly remarkable. To say I'm impressed is an understatement. We'd definitely like to move forward in this process with you. I'd like to schedule a time for you to meet with our search committee. Does next Tuesday night work for you?"

Kendall held back a chuckle. Aaron had literally not allowed her to get a word in, although now that she thought about it, Bob from First Church hadn't either. She readily agreed to the interview while at the same time relishing Aaron's affirmation of her teaching. In the years she'd been at Grace, never once had Nate actually seen her teach. Never once had he invited her to preach from his pulpit in worship, either. Not even on what she'd come to think of as "Youth Pastor Sunday"—the Sunday following Christmas when *every* youth pastor she knew preached, even those who weren't gifted teachers.

They worked out the details. It was only after Kendall hung up that she realized she'd met with Aaron before Trinity's search committee, something she found odd. She wondered what this said about Aaron's leadership, especially as she considered Jo's example of leadership with Hank.

Needing to process, she went upstairs and knocked softly on Frank's office door. "Can I come in?" she asked.

"Hold on just a few minutes," said Frank. "I'm finishing up some code. I'll come find you as soon as I'm done."

Kendall headed back downstairs and curled up in her prayer chair. She flipped open her Bible to Exodus 12, relieved that she'd finally finished the plagues. As she read through the story of the first Passover, these words from verse 24 leapt off the page:

You shall observe this rite as a perpetual ordinance for you and your children.

She'd never before paid attention to this particular part of the story. Here, early on in the story of God's people, God invited parents to disciple their children. Although this certainly occurred long before the days of professional youth ministry, she once again found herself thinking about both First Church and Trinity. She wondered if either actually entrusted and equipped parents to be the primary disciplers in their teens' lives.

As she was considering this, Frank walked in. "You look deep in thought," he said. "Should I head back upstairs or do you want to talk now?"

"I am deep in thought but I absolutely want to talk," Kendall said, motioning to the Ikea chair next to hers. "I just finished reading some more of Exodus. I can't even tell you how much this book is ministering to my soul right now, in some really unexpected ways. I'm noticing things I've never paid any attention to before."

"That's one of the beautiful things about Scripture, isn't it?" agreed Frank. "We can read the same stories over and over again and yet discover something new each and every time. You know I can talk about Scripture all day, but I've got just a few minutes before I've got to be on a call with a client. What's up?"

Kendall grinned. "I just wanted to fill you in on some developments."

"Good developments, I hope?"

"Definitely good developments. Bob called from First Church. They want me to move on in the process. And then Aaron called. He praised my teaching and wants me to move on in their process too. They both want follow-up interviews next week."

"That's fantastic, babe!" said Frank, reaching out to wrap Kendall in a big bear hug. "Congratulations! I'm so proud of you."

"But there is one thing," said Kendall hesitantly. "First Church wants references."

"Well, that won't be a problem for you," Frank assured her.

"That's true," replied Kendall. "But they want a reference from Grace."

"Oh. What are you going to do?"

"I was hoping you'd tell me."

"Wish I could. What are you thinking?"

"I feel like I have to be really careful about who I ask," Kendall said. "I don't want this news to spread before I'm ready for it to. I thought maybe I could ask Natalie. She's a parent but she's also one of my core leaders. She knows me well. I think she'd be genuinely happy for me about the prospect of starting somewhere that might offer me a bit more freedom and support."

"She'd be perfect, Kendall. Why don't you call her and try to meet with her this afternoon?"

"You mean I can't just send her an e-mail?" joked Kendall.

"You know you can't. You've got to do this in person."

"I know," said Kendall, fighting back tears. Frank headed back to his office while Kendall texted Natalie to see if she'd be available for coffee later that afternoon.

Thankfully, she was.

At 3 p.m., Kendall walked into the local Starbucks, where she took a break from her usual drink to order a Strawberry Frappuccino. She waved as Natalie walked in, looking slightly out of breath and a bit bedraggled, which was par for the course.

"Thanks for meeting with me on such short notice," Kendall said as Natalie sat down.

"Happy to," said Natalie. "But you should know I've only got thirty minutes before I've got to pick up Ava. So, you're on the clock. What can I do for you?"

Kendall knew Natalie well enough not to take offense at her briskness. "Well," she began, "I wanted to fill you in on something personal."

Kendall took a deep breath before updating Natalie on the events of the last few weeks. Knowing Grace would continue to be Natalie's church long after Kendall left, she took care not to say anything that might unnecessarily sour her toward Nate. When Kendall finished talking, Natalie blinked back tears. "I wish I could say I'm surprised but I'm not."

Kendall nodded.

"I'm so sad for Grace but I'm so happy for you, Kendall," Natalie said. "You're a gift. You've been a blessing to Grace. I have no doubt you'll be a blessing for whoever is lucky enough to hire you. Our loss is their gain, for sure."

"Thanks for saying that, Natalie. You know I love you and your entire family. And for what it's worth, nothing's for sure."

"Oh, I know," replied Natalie. "In the interest of full disclosure, I'm going to be praying that you don't get these jobs. Just kidding… maybe."

Kendall smiled and blinked back tears of her own. "There is one more thing," she said.

"Oh no!" grinned Natalie. "You can't possibly hit me with any more bad news today. I don't have the capacity to handle anything more!"

"It's not bad news," said Kendall quickly. "One of the churches I've been talking with, First Church, asked me for references. They'd like one of them to be from Grace. I was wondering if you'd be that reference for me?"

"I'd love to!" said Natalie, with an evil grin. "That way I can make sure you don't get the job!" She waited a beat. "You know I'm kidding, right, hon?"

"I think so…" said Kendall.

"I am," assured Natalie. "In all seriousness, it'd be a privilege to be a reference for you."

"Thanks."

Natalie stood up and held her arms out, waiting to envelop Kendall in a much-needed hug. "You are loved. By me—and God," whispered Natalie into Kendall's ear, repeating a phrase Kendall used all the time with The Lighthouse kids.

"You're such a mom," laughed Kendall. "You know I love that about you. For real though, thanks Natalie."

"Anytime," said Natalie. "But now I've gotta run and get Ava!"

"Say hi for me," said Kendall. "And please don't tell her—or anyone else—about this."

"It's not my news to tell," Natalie assured Kendall. "Your secret's safe with me."

As Kendall walked out of the coffee shop, she felt confident that it was.

From her car, Kendall e-mailed Bob with Natalie's contact information, along with that of her other two references, and then prayed, asking God for wisdom and clarity regarding her future.

■ ■ ■

SATURDAY, APRIL 25: ANOTHER MEETING WITH JAKE

Saturday morning, Kendall drove to The Perk to meet Jake. She ordered her usual and then settled into a booth in the back, careful to sit where she could see if anyone from Grace wandered in. While people from Grace were used to seeing her with Jake, she certainly didn't want anyone from her current church overhearing today's conversation. Once again, she couldn't help but feel as though she were cheating on Grace with someone else. That didn't feel good.

She flipped open her Bible to where she'd left off and again noticed the plagues. This time, something gave her pause. She marveled at Moses's courage to speak truth to power. This was a man with some serious gumption. Kendall thought again about her situation at Grace. Was she, too, being called to speak truth to power?

"Room for one more?" Jake asked as he slid into the booth with his tall black coffee.

"Always," Kendall said with a smile. "It's good to see you, Jake." She quickly caught him up on the events of the last few days.

"Wow!" Jake said. "I called it! You're about to get two offers!"

"Don't say that," whispered Kendall. "You'll jinx it!"

"Can't do that," Jake replied. "You know this is bigger than us. God's going to do what God's going to do."

"Stop with the Christian platitudes!" Kendall said playfully. "You know I can't stand those."

"Joking aside," said Jake, "tell me what you're currently thinking. Which way are you leaning?"

"Well, I'm trying not to lean either way," replied Kendall honestly. "I'm still not convinced I'm going to get these jobs."

"You always see the glass as half empty."

"One of us has to," laughed Kendall. "You always see it as full. Not half full—completely full."

"Like you said, one of us has to. But in all seriousness, what are you thinking?"

"Well…there's a lot I really like about both of these churches. First of all, I really like the senior pastors. Jo and Aaron both seem great, although I'll admit Aaron annoyed me quite a bit at first. He did grow on me though. I'd really love to work for a female senior pastor. I know I can't make a decision—if there is a decision to be made—based solely on gender, but as a female in youth ministry, it feels like such a unique opportunity to work with another woman."

"Hold on," interrupted Jake. "I want to go back to Aaron. Why did he annoy you initially?"

"He talked *a lot*. It took him quite a while to actually ask me any questions, which seemed strange, especially for an interview."

"Don't ignore your gut, Kendall. Listen to that. It's served you well in the past."

"I know…but I also can't make a decision based only on a feeling."

"You can't?" Jake asked with a smile. "Isn't that our ultimate goal in worship? To get you to feel the feeling?"

Kendall smiled, too. "It's not my goal," she replied honestly.

"I know. I just want to point out that now is not the time to be glossing over any red flags—feelings or otherwise."

"What do you mean by that?"

"When you're job searching, it can be so easy to play the comparison game with the churches you're looking at. You compare your worst— that idiot of a boss you work with—with what appears to be their best—Aaron and Jo. But during the interview process, everyone puts on their best front. You can't compare your worst to their best because you don't *really* know what their best is. For the record, you also don't really know what their worst is."

"What are you trying to say, Jake?" asked Kendall, a worried expression on her face.

"Just be careful. Don't brush off any bad feelings. Don't ignore any red flags. Dig deeper. Keep asking about your misgivings. Ultimately, you'll make a good, informed decision about fit and call when you compare your worst with another church's worst, or your best with another church's best."

"That makes sense. And you're right. I do compare my worst with another church's best a lot. That's not fair to anyone."

"Precisely," replied Jake.

"So, let's say that you're right and I end up with two offers. How do I decide which one to take?"

"You pray."

"You're kidding, right Jake?" asked Kendall. "Twenty-five years' experience in youth ministry and that's your advice for me?"

"Prayer and Jesus are always the right answer, Kendall. You know that," grinned Jake.

"But there's got to be more, right?" Whether she wanted to admit it or not, defaulting to *prayer* and *Jesus* made Kendall wary. She certainly believed in the power of both. Yet she'd learned in business school how to make good, informed choices. She wanted to do that here, especially if Jake was right and God's will really could be for her to end up at either church.

Once again, Jake seemed to read Kendall's mind.

"If you get two offers, you need to look at everything you know about both of them and analyze it. Consider call. Consider fit. Consider practical things like salary and benefits. And talk to Frank. This decision isn't just about you. It's also about him and your family. Where's he in all of this?"

"He's not thrilled," admitted Kendall. "Initially, he was irate. There's a chance I actually applied for these jobs before I talked to him."

"You didn't really do that, did you?" asked Jake in disbelief.

Kendall nodded. "I know. It was an awful thing to do. I was just so excited about what I found that I couldn't help myself."

"Kendall, you've got to remember that your marriage is more important than your ministry," warned Jake.

"I know!" said Kendall. "That's exactly what I told Frank."

"But that's definitely not what you showed Frank."

"You're right," said Kendall sheepishly. "I learned my lesson, though. I've been really up front about communicating with him ever since then."

"So what does Frank think about all this?"

"Ultimately, I think he really doesn't want to move. But I know he wants me to be happy."

"Of course he does," replied Jake. "Would either of these churches require you to move?"

"They're both local," said Kendall, a little too quickly.

"You know that's not what I meant..."

"I'm not sure," muttered Kendall. "We haven't actually had that conversation."

"I think you better," cautioned Jake. "Churches can be funny about that. Even if a commute seems doable to you, they might require their staff to live in their community."

"You're right," said Kendall, making a mental note to find this out from both places.

"On a slightly different note, there's something else I want to ask you," Jake said. "I've heard you question whether you'd go to Trinity or First Church. But what about Grace? Is your ministry done there?"

"I don't know." Kendall shrugged. "And I'm not just saying that. I honestly don't know. In so many ways, it would be easier for me to stay there. I know Grace. I know what's going to upset Nate, at least most of the time. I've got good adult leaders in place. I'm starting to develop good student leaders and I've got good relationships with my kids and most of their parents. There's no real reason why I couldn't stay for years."

When Jake looked at Kendall skeptically, she hurried to continue. "As you walked in, I was continuing to read Exodus. I keep getting pulled back to the plagues."

"Everyone's favorite story, right?" interjected Jake.

"As I was saying," smiled Kendall. "What jumped out at me wasn't the awfulness of the plagues. It's the way God called Moses to speak truth to power. What if that's what God's calling me to do at Grace?"

"Oh, so now you're Moses?" joked Jake. "Give me a break."

"I know I'm not Moses," laughed Kendall. "But you know what I mean, right?"

"I do," said Jake. "That's a nice way to rationalize why you should stay at Grace, but I'm still not convinced that's what God's actually calling you to do."

"Why?" questioned Kendall sincerely.

"Because I'm not sure staying is what's best for anyone," said Jake honestly.

"I've actually had that thought…more than once," said Kendall. "When Nate is screaming at me like a madman, I'm not at my best. He's certainly not at his best, either. In the last few weeks, I've begun to feel some release from this ministry. I have the sense that maybe I've done what God called me to do in this specific ministry. I've also had this sense of peace about leaving, almost like I've fulfilled my call at Grace."

"That's telling" said Jake. "Feelings of peace can be a good indication of what's going on internally. That sense that you've fulfilled your call at Grace is also telling, especially since I know your personality. There's always going to be more you *want* to do. But based on what you've told me, I'm not convinced there's more you *should* do."

"You always give me so much to think about, Jake. Thanks for that."

"Anytime, Kendall. I'm going to be on vacation next week, so let's talk in a few weeks, okay?"

"Absolutely!" agreed Kendall. "Who knows? Maybe at that point I'll even have two offers in hand and you can really help me choose!"

Kendall slid out of the booth and grabbed her and Jake's coffee cups to throw out.

She and Jake embraced before she ducked into her car, her mind spinning. Even though it was supposed to be her day off, Kendall had a bit of work to get done before Sunday. More importantly, she wanted to spend some time with Frank. Sometimes she had to remind herself that there was more to life than ministry. Much more.

And Frank was a big part of her much more.

■ ■ ■

TUESDAY, MAY 5: THE INTERVIEW AT TRINITY

As Tuesday came to a close and Kendall drove to her search committee interview at Trinity, she reflected on the past few days of ministry at Grace. Without a doubt, they'd been good.

On Sunday, she wrapped up the high school series on the trustworthiness of the Bible. She left impressed, encouraged by the way teens engaged with the series and asked good questions. She'd noticed an uptick in their willingness to dig into Scripture that seemed directly tied to the series.

Caden was a case in point. Ever since their conversation a few Sundays ago, Caden had been texting Kendall her questions about Scripture. Kendall encouraged Caden to write down those questions in a journal along with her observations about Scripture.

She knew whenever she saw Caden in person, she'd hear even more about her latest revelations. It was clear Caden's faith was growing by leaps and bounds.

These were the kinds of sweet moments Kendall savored. She was acutely aware she might not have many more of them with Caden or other teens from Grace.

Kendall also realized how little she'd seen Nate over the past couple of weeks. With stunning clarity, she concluded that when left to do her work alone, she and her ministry flourished. While she wanted to be a self-starter, she knew inherently that this was not good. Her best ministry should happen in partnership with her boss, not in spite of him or in his absence.

She was still thinking about this as Trinity came into view. Even though she'd already interviewed with Aaron, this was her first time at the church. It was a large, beautiful building on a busy intersection. She was surprised to notice a rundown looking collection of apartments across the street. Kendall wondered what the deal with them was, especially considering she was in an otherwise affluent suburb. She wondered if kids from those apartments attended programming at Trinity and if so, how parents felt about that.

As she had at First Church, she circled the building a few times before pulling into a nearby CVS (why was there literally a CVS on *every* corner?) to check her teeth and apply her lipstick. She gave herself a pep talk before putting the car into gear and heading back to the Trinity parking lot.

Unlike her experience at First Church, no one was outside to greet her. She grabbed her purse, shut the car door, and walked up to the building, trying to look more confident than she actually felt.

She was surprised to find the first door she tried locked. *What kind of church locks its building?* she wondered as she tried to find another entrance.

She saw a door on the other end of the building and headed that way. This experience wasn't giving her the best impression.

At the other end of the building, she found another locked door. This time, however, she noticed a doorbell to the left of the entrance. She pressed it. A few minutes later, Aaron appeared. "So sorry, Kendall. I meant to be outside waiting for you, but time got away from me today. You know how it goes."

Kendall nodded. She knew how easy it was for time to get away from you when you were focused on your work. It happened to her all the time. But she still wasn't sure it excused Aaron's not meeting her, especially since he claimed hospitality was one of his gifts.

Thinking about Jake's encouragement to examine red flags, Kendall decided to ask about the locked doors.

"You may have noticed the buildings across the street from us," Aaron said by way of explanation. "Sadly, it's an area of high crime in our little suburb. Our elders recently voted to keep our building locked up as an extra measure of security."

"Oh. You've had problems, then, with your neighbors?"

"Not at all," replied Aaron. "But we think the time to protect our building and staff is before something bad happens, not after."

Although she couldn't pinpoint exactly why, Aaron's answer made Kendall uncomfortable, perhaps because of how inhospitable it felt. Before she could ask a follow-up, Aaron motioned her forward, eager to change the subject.

"Let me give you the grand tour," he said.

For the next twenty minutes, Aaron showed Kendall around Trinity. It was a lovely, well-designed space that Kendall liked immediately.

As they wound their way up and down several sets of steps, Kendall realized she had no idea where she was in the building. She'd also yet to see any room filled with mismatched furniture. She braced herself, confident that as soon as they reached the youth room, she'd find such a space.

"Here we are," said Aaron finally. "The moment I'm sure you've been waiting for. This is our youth room."

Aaron pushed open a set of double doors.

Kendall couldn't help herself: She gasped. The room was bright and friendly, filled with windows and painted the loveliest shade of light blue. Instead of a hodgepodge of ripped and obviously discarded furniture, it was filled with new, comfy furniture, obviously chosen specifically for the space. On one side there was a coffee bar filled with teen-friendly snacks and drinks. Games were stacked in a corner. The walls were covered with canvas art. Curious, she asked Aaron about the artwork.

"Our teens designed them. We give each freshman one and ask them to decorate it. The first week of youth group, we have an art ceremony, where we add their new canvases to the wall. They hang for their four years of high school. As part of this ceremony, we ask each teen to share a bit about themselves and their canvas. Through that, we get to know them really well. Then, when they're a senior, we have another ceremony where we give them back their canvases and talk about how they came into our ministry as a blank canvas, contributed in powerful ways, and are leaving changed, in much the same way that they've changed our ministry."

"Wow," said Kendall. "That's really awesome. And I've got to tell you, I love this room. It's beautiful and welcoming."

"We worked hard on that. We want teens to want to be here. We want the space to feel safe to them and we're convinced you can't do that when you just give them everyone else's leftovers."

Feeling as though Aaron had read her mind, Kendall smiled, nodding her head in agreement.

"Let's go back upstairs to our conference room. That's where you'll meet our search committee."

Aaron led Kendall across the building to a well-appointed and beautifully laid out conference room. After ensuring Kendall had a drink, Aaron excused himself and let the search committee take over, which surprised Kendall. Since Aaron had pre-screened her, she had assumed he'd remain for her interview.

As Kendall glanced around the room, she was struck by the fact that there were no teens present. Sue, the head of the search committee, introduced herself and then quickly introduced everyone else. This search committee included Sue, a twenty-something who'd grown up in the church; Dave, a dad of a middle schooler; and three current high school leaders, none of whom had teens in the youth ministry themselves. It felt much less representative than First Church's search committee, a more authentic representation of actual stakeholders of the high school ministry.

For the next hour, the search committee asked Kendall a steady stream of questions, though no one read off a script. The interview felt less formal than the one at First Church and more conversational. She felt like she was dialoguing with five people who actually knew and understood youth ministry. They asked pointed questions. Sometimes, they challenged Kendall's responses. Kendall loved every minute of it.

As it felt like the interview was winding down, Dave asked a question. "Kendall, if you come here, we'd want this place to be more than just your job. We hope it would be your and Frank's church home. Given that, what would it look like for us to support you—not just in terms of your ministry, but personally as well?"

Kendall felt her eyes well up with tears. She realized just how unsupported she'd felt the last three years at Grace. That alone made her want to cry…as did the prospect of going somewhere that might actually offer her—and Frank—legitimate support.

"Wow," Kendall finally replied. "You caught me off guard with that question. Thanks so much for asking it. For me, support looks like affirmation. It looks like knowing what's going on in my ministry and asking what you can do to help—even if you're not one of my regular leaders. Support means having my back and speaking highly of our ministry to others in the congregation. Support means caring about Frank and me, not just because of what we bring to the ministry, but because of who we are. It means holding us in prayer and caring for us through the ups and downs of life."

"I think," said Dave, looking at the others on the search committee, "that you'll find that here. At least I hope you will. If you don't, I hope you'll come back to us and tell us how we can better support you.

We believe that ministry is a partnership. Too often, I think when we say that, most of us mean it's a 90/10 partnership. We don't. We truly want to partner with you in the faith formation of our teens in a way that feels equal and mutual."

"I love that, Dave. More than you probably realize. But I'm curious. If faith formation is really a partnership, where are all the teens? Why don't you have any on this committee?"

Kara, one of the adult leaders, quickly replied. "We thought long and hard about that. We really did. We talked to several other churches who are searching for youth pastors and learned that *all* of them included teens on their search committees. But to us, that felt like tokenism. We worried that a teen serving on this committee wouldn't actually feel heard and listened to and that it would end up being a negative experience for both them *and* the rest of the committee. So, we decided to take another approach. Rather than put a teen on this committee, we brought in a professional consulting company who ran a series of focus groups with our teens to pick their brains about the past and future of our youth ministry. That generated a pretty comprehensive list of values, all of which were created by our teens."

"Can I see those?" asked Kendall.

"Absolutely," said Sue. "I'll have Aaron e-mail them to you."

"I think that about covers it for today," said Dave. "It's been really good meeting with you. You'll hear from us by the end of the week. And if you have any more questions, just e-mail us." Dave handed Kendall a business card listing each group member's contact information.

Kendall stared at it in awe before she finally stood up and shook everyone's hands. A search committee business card? That was a first.

Sue walked her to her car.

"Thanks again," said Kendall as she got into her car. "This was great.

I'll look forward to hearing from you in a few days."

As usual, Kendall called Frank as soon as she got on the road.

"That was pretty awesome!" she said excitedly.

"That's great, babe! What was so awesome about it?"

"I don't even know where to begin. Let me just give you the highlights. The youth room has matching furniture and these incredible canvases. The space is thoughtful and welcoming and shows that this church actually values teens. The search committee was incredible. It was led by someone in their twenties! In their twenties, Frank, did you hear me? Not by a boomer!"

"Wow," replied Frank. "A church with young people who actually lead? Unicorns really do exist, eh?"

"Apparently! They had no teens on the search committee but that was because they had already brought in this professional group who did these focus groups with the teens to generate a list of values. They used those to anchor their search process. The whole thing felt pretty amazing. I think this could be it, Frank! This might actually be a church that really values its teens!"

"I'm so glad. I've got to be honest with you, Kendall. I know I'm not supposed to have favorites, but I've really been pulling for Trinity this whole time."

"Why?" asked Kendall, genuinely surprised to hear Frank say as much.

"You know that I've done okay at Grace, but to be honest, I'd like to be someplace that feels a little bit more like my home church," admitted Frank.

"What makes you think Trinity would feel more like home to you?" wondered Kendall.

"Well, I've done a little internet stalking of both Trinity and First Church since you started getting excited about them. In some ways, First Church reminds me a lot of Grace, which is a good thing. But Trinity just feels like the church I grew up in."

"Wow, babe," replied Kendall, carefully choosing her next words. "I'm really glad you told me this. I just wish you would have told me it sooner so your needs could have shaped my search a bit more."

"I appreciate that," said Frank. "But I know that the church world is weird and that there's not necessarily a lot of evangelical churches that will hire females. I sure don't want to be the one limiting your search more than it already is."

"I love you for that," replied Kendall. "But your preference is important, too. As you've told me, this change won't just affect me. It'll affect both of us."

"Yes, it will," agreed Frank. "We'll keep processing this, but for now, can you please just come home so we can watch *Parks and Rec?*"

"You bet!" Kendall grinned. "As long as I can have a margarita while we watch it!"

"Absolutely," said Frank, who greeted her at the door with one.

■ ■ ■

WEDNESDAY, MAY 6: A STUDY IN CONTRASTS

As the alarm went off, Frank rolled over so that when Kendall opened her eyes, he was the first thing she saw.

"AHHH!" she screamed playfully.

"You ready for the day?" Frank asked.

"Not until I have my breakfast Pepsi."

"That's a nasty habit."

"I know," said Kendall. "But right now, I don't care. Just give me the caffeine."

"Why can't you drink coffee like a normal person?" joked Frank.

After lying in bed for a few glorious minutes, Kendall finally got ready for work before heading downstairs to grab some apple cinnamon oatmeal and her much-coveted Pepsi.

"You eating here or heading out?" inquired Frank.

"Heading out," replied Kendall. "Don't forget, today's going to be crazy. I've got the interview with the board at First Church at 4 p.m. I'm going to try to come home after for dinner, but if the interview goes long, I'll have to go straight to church. It's senior night."

"It's sure going to be an interesting day for you," remarked Frank, knowing she was about to combine the stress of an interview with one of her favorite nights of the year: senior night, when they recognized and honored all the high school graduates and their families.

"It will definitely be quite a day," agreed Kendall. "See you later."

Because of her interview later that night, she drove the four blocks to Grace. She pulled in just as Nate arrived.

"Kendall," he said as they walked in together. "It feels like it's been a long time since we've chatted. Got a minute to connect this morning?"

Even though she didn't, she found herself nodding yes to Nate's request. "Want to meet me in my office?" she asked hopefully.

"Why don't you come to mine?" requested Nate, as usual.

Knowing that some things weren't worth the fight, Kendall dropped off her bags in her office before heading to Nate's. The closer she got, the more dread she felt. That dread, she realized, had been her constant companion in every encounter she'd had with Nate since the blowup with Jill. She wondered if it would ever go away.

Finding Nate's office door open, Kendall walked in and took her usual seat as she waited for him to finish sending an e-mail. How he'd managed to start working on something during the four minutes it had taken her to get to his office was incomprehensible to her.

Eventually, Nate turned his attention to her. Never one to waste words on small talk—at least not with Kendall—he dove in.

"I wanted to let you know I had another call from a parent," Nate began.

Oh crap, thought Kendall. Thankfully, she filtered her inner monologue and instead questioned, "And?"

"Thought we better talk about it," replied Nate. "This one came from Caden's parents."

Kendall mentally reviewed the last several weeks, trying to figure out what she'd done to upset them. She couldn't come up with anything. From her vantage point, Caden was more involved in The Lighthouse than she'd ever been. She did, however, remember Caden saying her parents were a little uneasy that they were talking about the trustworthiness of Scripture at The Lighthouse. Kendall decided this must be what their call to Nate was about.

"They appear to be your biggest fans," Nate continued, surprising Kendall. "They told me all about this series you're doing on the trustworthiness of the Bible, including how skeptical they were of what you were teaching the kids. They think you've done a tremendous job and are thrilled by how Caden is digging into Scripture. They thought it was really important for me to know that. I, in turn, think it's really important for you to know."

"Thanks," said Kendall tentatively, confident that a "but" must still be coming.

"I know we've experienced some conflict the last few weeks," resumed Nate. "I wanted you to know how grateful I am for your ministry here at Grace. You've been a real asset to our church."

Kendall had a hard time not staring at Nate in open-mouthed wonder. Where had her real boss gone? Instead, she simply said, "Thanks, Nate. I really appreciate that."

After a beat, she continued. "Is there something else?"

"Nope, that's it."

"Okay, then," said Kendall awkwardly. She pushed her chair back, got up, and raced down the hall, trying to wrap her mind around what had just happened.

Bolstered by Nate's encouragement, Kendall worked quickly through her to-do list the rest of the morning. She was acutely aware of how few hours she had to accomplish the day's tasks before she'd need to leave for her interview at First Church.

As Kendall drove to First Church later that afternoon, she prayed for wisdom and clarity. She also found herself reliving her previous interview at First Church and in particular her interaction with Hank, the board chair. She wondered whether Hank would be there today and worried what their interaction would be like if he was.

When she arrived, she was surprised to see Bob, not Jo, waiting for her. Bob welcomed her warmly and thanked her for her references, saying how much he and Jo had enjoyed talking with them.

Bob led Kendall into the church building and ushered her into a conference room, much less well-appointed than the one at Trinity. She immediately noticed Hank, mustered her courage, and went over to him, shaking his hand. He welcomed her warmly.

Bob and Hank then introduced her to the remaining elders. There was Peg, a seventy-something longtime member of the congregation; Sophie, a young professional who was also their treasurer; Sam, a fifty-something corporate lawyer who served as their secretary; Cliff, a twenty-something who'd grown up in the church, went away to college, and returned to their suburban community after marrying his high school sweetheart; and Olivia, a forty-something stay-at-home mom. Kendall couldn't help but notice that like First Church's search committee, their elders represented every group within the congregation—except, she realized, teenagers.

Hank offered Kendall a glass of water, which she eagerly took before sitting down in the chair he directed her toward, which was at the head of the conference table. *Nothing like being in the hot seat*, she thought to herself.

Before long, the interview began. This one was far less choreographed than her first interview with the search committee. Members of the board asked her about the role of worship in forming youth, about what intergenerational ministry meant to her, about how she collaborated with colleagues, and, most interestingly, about how she mentored leaders.

Considering she'd been less than impressed with how the search committee answered her questions regarding what a healthy follower of Jesus looked like, she was surprised when the board seemed very interested in her willingness to build a team to disciple teens. Sensing there was a story here, she asked a question. "You've been asking me a lot about how I'd disciple adult leaders. I'm curious, how have your youth ministry's leaders traditionally been discipled?"

The board looked around at one another before Olivia answered. "I feel like I'm the person best equipped to respond to that since my daughters are both in the high school ministry. To be honest, that's been a gap. Our last two youth pastors, Paul and Chad, were both energetic. You might even say they were teen magnets who could draw a crowd because teens LOVED being around them. Initially, we thought that was really good, important even. But what we realized after Paul and Chad left is that neither one built a team of adult leaders to support their ministry. When they left, our youth ministry was worse off than before. It collapsed. Our teens no longer wanted to come because their connection had been with Paul and Chad, not with each other, or, more importantly, with God."

Reading between the lines, Kendall asked another question. "So, whoever you hire is walking into a situation in which they're going to be building a leadership team from scratch. Is that correct?"

Olivia nodded but said, "Sort of. I think you met Sarah during your interview with our search committee. She's been a parent volunteer for quite a while in our youth ministry. I think she'd like to continue serving but feels really ill-equipped to do so. She wants to be mentored and discipled so that she can lead well. I think you'll find that there are other Sarahs in our midst, too."

This need matched well with Kendall's gifts of leadership, teaching, and even hospitality. She asked a follow-up. "As a board, I'm curious, what would your priority for the next youth pastor be: To disciple every teenager—or to build a team of adult leaders capable of doing that?"

Once again, the board looked at one another, as if communicating via some unspoken, secret language. Cliff, the twenty-something who'd grown up in the church, spoke on their behalf. "I was in the youth ministry during Paul's tenure and I can say with confidence that we want you to disciple adults who will then disciple our teens. As a congregation, we've been doing a church-wide study on the life of the apostles this spring. We've been talking a lot about leaders who multiply their ministry, like Jesus did with the apostles. That's what we want the next youth pastor to be: a multiplier."

Kendall felt a whoosh of excitement rush over her. This seemed to fly in the face of what Hank had said at her last interview about the importance of numbers. She thought for a second about Jake's encouragement to probe any red flags she saw and decided if she was seriously going to consider working at First Church, she had to gain clarity about what she'd heard previously. Although she knew it was risky, she decided to put Hank on the spot.

"I'm really encouraged by what Cliff just said," began Kendall. "I think that's the best way to form teens' faith. But I need to revisit something Hank said at my other interview. Hank, you said the success of the next youth pastor would be evaluated based on numbers. But that doesn't necessarily fit with what I'm hearing today. Can you clarify?"

"Absolutely," replied Hank, much more calmly than she expected. "I actually *do* think it fits. If a youth pastor comes to First Church and does exactly what Cliff described, I expect our numbers to increase. The more leaders who are equipped for ministry, the more youth you can effectively disciple. Part of the reason why our youth ministry's numbers have remained stagnant for so long is that it became a cult of personality. The kids who kept coming were the ones who liked Paul and Chad. Teens who didn't connect with them just left. I don't think that will be the case for someone who truly leads by discipling others."

Kendall couldn't suppress her grin.

Hank noticed. "I see that resonates with you, yes?"

"It really does," said Kendall honestly. "I do have one other question. You guys asked me a lot today about the role of intergenerational worship in forming the faith of teens and about how I collaborate with colleagues. How do you envision your new youth pastor fitting into the overall life of the church?"

"Can you tell us more about what you mean by that?" asked Peg.

"Sure. What would my role be in planning weekend worship services for the whole congregation? Would I have one?"

As if connected by some invisible string, every single board member nodded their head *yes*. "Absolutely, Kendall," Sophie said. "Bob passed around the curriculum sample you sent and Jo shared a video of your teaching from your YouTube page. We think you're a gifted teacher. If you come to First Church, we'd like to design a role for you where your primary role would be youth pastor but where you'd also have worship responsibilities. We'd like you to preach and teach in our main worship services at least four times a year. Going forward, we believe that is an important part of intergenerational ministry. We want all of our adults to get to know you in that way—even if they never interact with our youth ministry. We also want our teens to know and be close to someone on our teaching team."

"That's okay with Jo?" asked Kendall hesitantly, thinking that Nate would never allow for such a thing.

"Are you kidding?" laughed Sophie. "It was her idea!"

"Oh wow," responded Kendall, at a bit of a loss for words. Thankfully, Hank chose that moment to check his watch and suggest they end in prayer.

Hank walked Kendall to her car. "We're in the process of doing final interviews with our last couple of candidates," he explained. "We're hoping someone will be in place before fall programming begins. You can expect to hear from us in the next couple of weeks. Please feel free to reach out in the meantime with other questions."

"Thanks," said Kendall. "I'll look forward to hearing from you. This was really good tonight, Hank. I'm so thankful to have engaged in this process with your congregation."

"Us too," said Hank with a smile. "Have a good rest of your night. I know from Bob that you're headed back to run the youth ministry tonight at Grace. I imagine that will be a bit challenging emotionally. You'll be in our board's prayers."

"Thanks," said Kendall, unsure what else to say as she closed the car door, thankful for their prayers and eager to be alone with her thoughts.

As Kendall drove, she realized she was liking First Church more and more. She was so intrigued by what she'd heard tonight, especially by the idea that there would be room for her to use her gifts to shepherd the whole congregation. That felt like authentic intergenerational ministry in a way that nothing else had. She wondered if she'd be allowed to do that at Trinity. She made a mental note to ask Aaron the next time they spoke.

As she drove, she mentally prepared herself to lead youth group. She was already physically exhausted, and Hank was right. She was mentally exhausted, too. But she knew senior night was important. Thankfully, her program was already planned. She'd interview each senior about their time at The Lighthouse as well as their future plans. Then their small group leader would speak, as would a significant adult in their life and one student leader, who would present them with an award that recognized them for the gifts they'd brought to The Lighthouse during their tenure there. Then they'd lay hands on and pray for each senior individually.

Senior night was always a good, albeit emotional, experience. But as she thought about the night ahead, she couldn't help but wonder what such a night would look like at Trinity, when each senior would also receive the canvas that had adorned the youth room during their high school career. She loved that idea and suspected she'd borrow it, regardless of whether or not she ended up there.

After calling Frank to let him know the interview had run long and she wouldn't have time to stop at home for dinner, she went through the drive-through at Chick-fil-A and ordered a Cobb Salad, no egg, along with a large fry and lemonade.

Once at Grace, she set up for the night, grabbing bites of her salad between running in and out of the youth room to get various needed items. She put out extra chairs for the parents of seniors, whom she'd invited to join them. After setting up, she took a minute to pray for their night before sitting down and collecting herself.

Before she knew it, it was 6:30 and her adult leaders walked in, eager to talk through the flow of the night and go over their responsibilities. Kendall quickly reviewed everything, pleased that her adults would have a lot of stage time in front of the parents.

Twenty-five minutes later, teens started to arrive. Caden got there first. She came right up to tell Kendall about her latest foray into Scripture.

"I've been reading Exodus," began Caden, as Kendall repressed a smile. *Why is everyone I know currently reading Exodus?* she wondered. *What are you trying to tell me, God?*

"When we did our trustworthiness of the Bible series, we talked about how important it was to understand who the author is when we're reading Scripture," said Caden. "All my life, I've been taught that Moses wrote Exodus. But if Moses wrote it, why doesn't he refer to himself in the first person? If he didn't write it, then why does everyone think he did? Does that change anything?"

Encouraged by all of Caden's questions and the enthusiasm with which she was approaching Scripture, Kendall couldn't hold back her smile anymore. Unfortunately, a quick look at her watch revealed that it was 6:59, so Kendall arranged to meet Caden the next day after school to talk more.

Kendall turned her attention to the seniors, careful to greet each one's family as they arrived. At 7:05, Natalie went onstage to greet everyone. She welcomed parents and seniors as well as the rest of the teens before inviting the first senior, Jonathan, to come forward. Kendall interviewed Jonathan before calling up Jonathan's small group leader and dad to speak. Finally, Kayla, one of their student leaders, gave Jonathan the award for the person most likely to walk away from time with his friends to welcome a newbie into The Lighthouse.

The night proceeded without a hitch. As senior after senior was called forward, Kendall found herself counting her blessings. These were the kids she'd met when they were sophomores and poured into every day since. In many ways, they were "hers" and she was grateful for every one of them. She fought back tears as she watched leaders and parents speak into their lives.

She tried not to wonder what this night might look like next year if she wasn't there. In that moment, though, she realized that while it would look different, she'd equipped a solid group of leaders to do ministry. If tonight was any indication, they'd be fine. She hadn't been up front except for the interviews and to lay hands on each of their twelve seniors. Sure, she'd close out the night and thank everyone for coming, but she felt like she was doing that because it was expected of her, not because someone else couldn't do it.

As Kendall watched her adult leaders, her thoughts drifted to the adult leaders (or lack thereof) at Trinity and First Church. At yesterday's interview, she'd met three of the core leaders at Trinity. She'd liked them all and suspected she'd enjoy working with them. In contrast, if she went to First Church, she'd be building a team from scratch, starting with Sarah, who, based on what the board had said, was eager to learn and be equipped.

Now, as Kendall watched her adult leaders do what she'd trained them to do, she realized how much the situation at First Church reminded her of what she'd inherited at Grace. First Church's Sarah was like Grace's Natalie—a parent who wanted to be involved but lacked the training and confidence necessary to flourish in ministry.

At Grace, Natalie had been enough of a starting point for Kendall to build a great team of leaders. She'd been one of those adult leaders from that very first, nearly disastrous mission trip. When Natalie had decided to give Kendall a chance and keep serving, so had many of the other leaders from that trip. Ever since then, she'd poured into them. The result was this incredible team she sat in awe of tonight.

In some ways, she realized, she was more troubled about the prospect of leaving her leaders than she was about leaving her students. She wondered what that said about her as a youth pastor. Before she could figure it out, Natalie called her to the stage to close out the evening.

After saying her final words, Kendall walked around the room, hugging the seniors and affirming their parents. What she really wanted to do was fall to the couch, exhausted. As the room cleared out, she thanked her adult leaders for all they'd done. Together they cleaned up the youth room and locked the building.

By the time Kendall got home, she was completely and utterly exhausted.

Frank took one look at her and surmised, "I bet you have a lot to tell me...but I bet you need some time to just be. Just give me one word or phrase to tell me how tonight went."

Despite her exhaustion, Kendall couldn't help but chuckle at how Frank turned one of her most common processing questions back around to her.

She sighed. "It was emotionally exhausting but God-honoring."

"Good enough," replied Frank. "You know I want to hear more about it...and the rest of your day...and the job search, but I know you're exhausted. How about we put this conversation on hold until our date night on Friday? Remember, I've got in-office meetings for the next two days and tomorrow I won't be home until late."

Kendall nodded her head in agreement, relieved Frank understood how much she needed a little space after such an emotional night. She headed upstairs to soak in the tub, thankful for the time to collect her thoughts after such a good but tumultuous day.

Two weeks ago, after her initial round of interviews at First Church and Trinity, she'd felt such clarity. She wanted to work at Trinity.

Now, after the second round of interviews, she wasn't so sure. As much as she liked Trinity, she was starting to see herself at First Church more.

To further complicate things, Kendall kept replaying her earlier conversation with Nate about Caden's parents. The conversation had felt different—so different—than any other she'd had with him. That combined with the euphoria of senior night left Kendall questioning whether her work at Grace was not yet finished. She wondered if she had more options than she'd originally thought. Maybe she didn't just need to choose between First Church and Trinity. Maybe she also needed to seriously consider staying.

■ ■ ■

THURSDAY, MAY 7: ICE CREAM WITH CADEN

Not surprisingly, Kendall slept later than usual on Thursday morning.

After the sheer exhaustion of the day before, she was thankful she had a fairly unscheduled day until her meeting with Caden that afternoon. As Kendall worked on mission trip prep and various tasks for the next gathering at The Lighthouse, she found herself seriously contemplating staying at Grace. She was still thinking about this as she headed to Baskin-Robbins to meet with Caden.

After grabbing their Rainbow Sherbet and Daquiri Ice, Caden and Kendall sat down and talked about their days. "I'm so impressed with how you've been digging into Scripture, Caden." Kendall said after they'd caught up a bit. "I love your enthusiasm for God's Word!"

Caden smiled. "I've got to admit," she began, "I've been really surprised by how much I'm enjoying reading the Bible. My parents have tried for *years* to get me to have a daily quiet time. They kept telling me it'd be good for me. But the more they told me to do it, the less I wanted to. You know how that goes."

"I do," laughed Kendall. "What finally clicked for you? Why are you enjoying it so much?"

"Like I've said before, it's been this series we've been doing at The Lighthouse. It's changed how I see the Bible. I'm now approaching it with this sense of wonder. I have so many questions! It's like my questions are contagious. The more I have, the more I want to keep reading in order to try to figure out the answers. But that just gets exhausting after a while. So, I thought I'd ask you my questions instead."

Kendall laughed. Caden's experience with questions and exploring Scripture was eerily similar to her own. "What questions do you have for me today?"

"Can we start with the one I asked you yesterday? Who wrote Exodus?"

"Who do you think wrote Exodus?"

"That's not fair!" Caden grumbled. "You can't just turn my question back around on me!"

"Sure I can!" Kendall teased with a smile. "Seriously, though. Who do you think wrote it?"

"Like I said," said Caden, "I've always been told it's Moses. But the more I read it, the stranger that seems."

"Why?"

"Because Moses is consistently referred to in the third person," replied Caden. "If Moses actually wrote Exodus, wouldn't he have written it like an autobiography? I mean, I'd never write about myself by saying, 'Caden saw a burning bush.' Why would Moses write that?"

"That's a really great point," agreed Kendall. "Long story short. We don't know for sure who wrote Exodus. During the time of the Exodus, stories were told orally, passed down from one generation to the next. It's possible Moses had a hand in that. It's also possible he didn't."

"If we don't know who wrote Exodus, then how can we trust it?" asked Caden, returning to the root of her question.

"Do we have to know exactly who wrote something in order to trust it?" asked Kendall.

"Well, I sure think it helps!" muttered Caden. "It's like we learn in history. Sources lend credibility to their writing."

"Absolutely!" Kendall agreed. "That's true of the Bible, too. In fact, I think that's probably one of the reasons why we've so often attributed Exodus to Moses. If Moses wrote it, then of course it's trustworthy."

"That makes a lot of sense," admitted Caden.

"But I think we can still trust Exodus, even if we don't know for sure that Moses wrote it."

"What do you mean?" asked Caden, genuinely puzzled.

"You've heard that the Bible was inspired by God, right?"

"Yep," agreed Caden. "I think I've even heard that from you once or twice."

"Probably," said Kendall, smiling. "To me, that means that God was involved in every aspect of the Bible: God was involved in its writing, in deciding which books were put in the Bible and which ones were left out, and even in the Bible's repeated translations. What we have in the Bible is exactly what God wanted us to have."

"That makes sense," Caden said. "Even if it does seem a little simplistic."

"You're right," said Kendall. "It does seem simplistic. So, try this. Read Exodus as though Moses wrote it. What questions would that raise for you? Then read it as if someone else wrote it. What questions would that raise for you?"

"Oh, I like that. It's almost like I can test out some different theories."

"Exactly!" agreed Kendall. "And if this issue really bothers you, let me give you some articles about what some Bible scholars say about who wrote Exodus. Spoiler alert: They don't all agree with one another."

"That's helpful, actually," admitted Caden.

"Say more," invited Kendall.

"Well, it's helpful to know that not everyone agrees with each other on this issue. That makes me feel like I don't have to have it totally figured out either."

"Absolutely! The Bible can still teach us—even as we wrestle with it. Speaking of which, what else are you wrestling with?"

"Let me show you my list," replied Caden. She then grabbed her Bible, opened it to the first page of Exodus and proceeded to produce a list of at least twenty questions scribbled in the margins, including:

- Why did God allow the Israelites to become slaves?
- If God heard the cries of God's people, why'd it take God so long to do anything about it?
- Where's my burning bush? What's God calling me to do?
- How can we root for God during the final plague? Is God evil for slaughtering so many innocent people?

"Wow," replied Kendall. "Those are some really great questions! I love how you're asking things about the stories themselves as well as things about what those stories mean for you. I'm also so glad you're writing your questions down. You know what else I think you should do?"

"What?"

"Get a journal. Start recording your questions there…along with any answers you find. I think you'll be amazed at the way God shows up in your search. I'm happy to keep meeting with you and talking through your questions, too."

As soon as Kendall said that, she hesitated. Could she really make that promise to Caden when she was knee-deep in interviewing at two other churches, secretly hoping she'd get a job offer elsewhere?

She wasn't sure she could, but unfortunately, the words were already out of her mouth. Unable to retract them, she continued, hoping Caden wouldn't notice her sudden awkwardness. "I mean, I don't know that I'll always be able to answer your questions, but I'm always happy to talk about them with you."

"I'd like that," said Caden, just as her phone dinged. She motioned to her screen. "My mom's here!" Caden grabbed her stuff, thanked Kendall for the ice cream, and headed out the door.

After she left, Kendall buried her head in her hands and sobbed.

How could she leave Grace?

For the first time, she found herself praying she wouldn't get *either* offer and that the choice between Trinity and First Church that she'd longed for would actually elude her. She also flashed back to her conversation with Nate the day before. She wondered if perhaps Nate was changing, too. After his conversation with Caden's parents, maybe he'd finally realized that for every Jill, there was also someone who loved and respected her work, that she was a valuable part of ministry at Grace. Maybe if she just tried harder, she could mend and even restore her relationship with Nate.

Maybe she needed to try, for the sake of Caden and her kids at Grace.

■ ■ ■

FRIDAY, MAY 8:
A MUCH-NEEDED CONVERSATION WITH FRANK

When she went downstairs to grab her breakfast Pepsi on Friday, she found a note from Frank, saying how excited he was for their date night at their favorite steak place, especially after a rare two days of virtually no conversation between them.

Midway through her day, the phone rang. It was Aaron. She picked up, fearing she was about to hear the rejection she'd been expecting ever since she started interviewing at Trinity. Instead, Aaron said, "Just wanted to check in with you, Kendall. I was curious if you had any additional questions for us as you enter your own discernment process."

Kendall was touched. "Thanks for checking in, Aaron. Actually, I do have a question for you. Both you and the search committee have been very affirming of my teaching gifts. I'm wondering how, if at all, you'd see me using them to serve the broader church?"

Aaron paused.

To Kendall, the silence felt like an eternity. In reality, it was about five seconds.

"I've got to be honest with you, I hadn't really considered that," said Aaron. "Traditionally at Trinity, our youth pastor's focus has been on the youth ministry, not on contributing to *big church*, as we like to call it."

Kendall suspected that Aaron was trying to be funny, but still, something rubbed her the wrong way about his use of the phrase *big church.* Remembering what Jake had told her about the importance of probing red flags, she pushed. "But didn't you say that you were committed to having youth actively serve in worship?"

"Oh, we are!" replied Aaron enthusiastically. "Really, that's how you'd contribute to big church, by encouraging the teens to participate."

"So, despite my teaching gifts, you don't think there would be an opportunity for me to preach in worship?" questioned Kendall, deciding then and there that she'd never say *big church.*

"Well, never say never," Aaron replied. "I suppose we might be able to put you in the preaching schedule the Sunday after Christmas, when the stakes are a little less."

Although Kendall suspected Aaron thought he was throwing her a bone, his comments felt belittling, especially since earlier he'd been so effusive with his praise for her teaching. Either he thought she was gifted and good enough to preach in worship, or he didn't actually think she was gifted. Unsure how to respond, she simply waited, confident that Aaron would fill the silence.

After a few seconds, Aaron continued, backpedaling a bit. "I guess what I'm trying to say, Kendall, is if that's important to you, we can keep talking about it after you get here. I'm confident we can work out something that will be agreeable to us both."

Kendall wasn't so sure. She felt Aaron had brushed off her sincere question. The feeling was all too familiar to her after years of Nate doing the same.

After some more pleasantries and small talk, Kendall reminded Aaron to send her the values the teens had created in connection with the consultants they'd hired. Shortly after hanging up, she received Aaron's e-mail. The values read:

- We value each other. We love one another, actively try to get to know one another, and respect one another.

- We value our faith. We love Jesus and want to learn how to be more like him. We think we can do that best when we're together.

- We value service. We're passionate about injustice and believe that together, we can actually do something to fix what's broken in our world…or at least in our community.

- We value diversity. We know we're not all alike and are mostly okay with that. We know that God created us this way and that we each reflect something uniquely awesome about God.

- We value questions. We ask questions to learn more about each other, Jesus, and our faith.

Kendall couldn't help smiling as she read. The values felt honest but reflective of so many teens she knew, even at Grace. The list also seemed to support a faith that was a bit deeper than that of the kids she'd met at First Church, which was exciting. Kendall knew that kind of faith wasn't developed in a vacuum. It reflected highly on the adult leadership structure that was in place at Trinity.

For the rest of the afternoon, Kendall worked furiously before heading home to change for her date night with Frank.

After checking in at the restaurant and learning that Frank was not yet there, Kendall took a seat at the bar and ordered a frozen strawberry margarita. She mentally reviewed everything she wanted to talk to Frank about. Before long, Frank walked up behind her, kissing her neck and greeting her.

Once seated, they ordered their usual—a chopped salad to share and a well-done filet encrusted in blue cheese with a side of potatoes au gratin. Frank ordered the same, except with his meat bloody.

As they waited for their food to arrive, Frank looked at Kendall expectantly. "Tell me everything," he invited.

Kendall forced herself to pause and first ask Frank about his day. She feared that once she started talking, Frank wouldn't be able to get a word in.

Frank happily filled her in on what had gone well in his presentation with his client as well as some members of his team that he was struggling with. "Thanks for asking, babe. But we both know your life is more interesting right now. Tell me about Wednesday."

"Well," said Kendall. "First of all, you know it's *our* life right?"

"I know, babe," said Frank with a smile. "I'm just giving you a hard time."

"That's important though, Frank," said Kendall. "Jake actually called me on this a while ago. He warned me not to get too far ahead of you in this process. Am I? I mean, I know this is my career but it's our life. It's our church. Are you really ready to leave Grace?"

Frank chuckled. "I really appreciate you asking me. But you should know better than anyone, even though I'm not necessarily thrilled about the idea of moving, I've been ready to leave Grace for a long time. I'm tired of how Nate treats you. I want to see what God does with you if you're in a place where your boss actually has your back."

Frank looked at Kendall, who had just opened her mouth to speak. "Don't even try to defend him," pleaded Frank. "I know I've tried to find the best in him in the past, but let's not get carried away. He may be one hell of a preacher, but that's not enough. That's not actually what makes someone a good pastor."

"I know," sighed Kendall. "But I've got to tell you about this conversation I had with him on Wednesday. It was so different from any conversation I've ever had with him. Long story short: Caden's parents called and told him how much they've appreciated my ministry with Caden. Nate was grateful and even affirming of my ministry. He didn't exactly apologize for the thing with Jill but he came so close. The whole thing made me wonder if he's changing. Maybe I need to try harder to make things work at Grace."

"Whoa!" cautioned Frank. "Slow down. If Nate changed, would that make you want to stay?"

"I think so," Kendall said slowly.

"Do you think Nate's really changed, though?" asked Frank. "I mean, it seems pretty easy to communicate value to someone after someone else has just reminded you how awesome they are. It seems to me that Nate should be able to see how awesome your ministry is all on his own. He shouldn't need Caden's parents to tell him that. He should know that from working with you."

"You might be right," replied Kendall. "But that's not the only thing that makes me feel like maybe I should stay. Yesterday, I had such a great conversation with Caden. She's learning and growing in her faith so much, Frank! How can I leave at such a pivotal moment?"

"Aren't you the one who's always said that a teen's faith shouldn't depend on you?" retorted Frank.

"Well, yes." Kendall took a deep breath. "But it's not just Caden. In so many ways, my ministry here is still in its infancy. What if God's not done with me here yet?"

"Hmm," considered Frank. "It's interesting. When you asked me if I was ready to leave Grace, all I could think about was your relationship with Nate. I've been ready to leave that for a long time. What gives me pause are my friendships with Andy and Pete. I know they're your leaders, but they're my friends. I don't want to leave them."

Kendall paused, carefully choosing her next words.

"Thanks for telling me that," she said. "But you know that if we leave Grace, your relationships with Andy and Pete don't have to end, right?"

"I thought you might say that," Frank replied with a sad smile. "And you're right. But you're also wrong. My relationships with Andy and

Pete are rooted in church. So sure, they can continue if we leave. But they won't be the same. I know that's true for your relationships too, but it also feels a little different. I worry that every time we start over, I'm going to be more reluctant to form new relationships with people at church because I've learned the hard way that they're fleeting; that they're entirely dependent on your job status. That's really hard."

"It is," said Kendall, her eyes filling with tears. "I had no idea that's how you were feeling. I am so sorry, babe. Maybe we should stay."

"It would certainly be easier," admitted Frank. "But I'm not sure that easier is always best. So why don't you tell me about the other day? How did it go with First Church?"

"It was so good." Kendall was surprised at the positive emotion she still felt, despite how genuinely conflicted she was starting to feel about the possibility of staying. "In fact, it surprised me how good it was. Before last night, had you asked me which church I wanted to work for, I would have said Trinity, hands down, especially since I know that's also your preference. And I don't know, maybe that church still makes sense. Aaron sent me the values the kids created. They're amazing. And I'd love to work with teens who already have a solid faith foundation. On paper, they're perfect. But I don't know, Frank, I'm not sure they'd be perfect for me or even for us."

"What do you mean?" asked Frank curiously.

"Well, initially I thought I was really going to like Aaron. Or let me rephrase. Initially, I liked the idea of Aaron and being led by someone closer to my age. But there's something about him that makes me uncomfortable. Even though I can't quite put my finger on it, it's enough to make me feel like I don't know if I'd love working with him. He did call earlier today though to see how my discernment was going."

"That's good, right?" questioned Frank, trying hard to make Kendall see the bright side of Trinity. "You love people who process things!"

"I do," agreed Kendall. "But during our conversation, I asked him what he thought my role in worship might be. He responded by calling it *big church*."

"Oh," said Frank. "I'm guessing that phrase didn't sit well with you."

"It didn't," admitted Kendall. "It's just inherently derogatory. It shouldn't be used. But that issue aside, he basically brushed me off and said we'd figure it out later. That really rubbed me the wrong way. Plus, I don't even know if I mentioned this to you, but I had such a hard time getting into Trinity's building the other night. Every single door I tried was locked. When I asked Aaron about it, he said the church is preemptively taking measures to protect its staff. But Frank, there's a rundown apartment building directly across the street from Trinity. I can't help but wonder if there are folks living there who aren't white and if Aaron and the people at Trinity are freaked out by that."

"Oh, wow," said Frank. "That would definitely be worrisome. You need to find out."

"I know," agreed Kendall. "I just haven't figured out how to broach the issue yet. I will, though."

"But what about First Church, then? We started there and then ended up talking about Trinity. Tell me more about the interview with their board."

"It was really good." Kendall recounted the highlights. "I keep coming back to what Jake said about fit."

"What do you mean?"

"I mean, on paper, First Church is actually a little bit of a disaster," replied Kendall, somewhat cautiously. "But they've got heart. And I'm really good at the things they need. I think I could be a real asset not just to their youth ministry but to their church. That's another thing, Frank. Their board said that I'd have the chance to preach in worship at least four times a year because it's obvious that teaching is one of my gifts—and they want me to be able to use my gifts to benefit the *whole* church!"

"Well, that's certainly a direct contrast to Aaron's reaction to your gifts, isn't it?"

Kendall agreed. "It is. I really think I'd be able to serve the whole church at First Church. And I think I'd like working with Jo. I'd be excited to lead their youth ministry because their needs align exactly with my gifts. I really think I'd be able to grow their ministry."

"Huh," laughed Frank. "Isn't that what you were all upset about after your first interview? Wasn't Cliff a little obsessed with growth?"

Kendall smiled. "Hank, not Cliff. Cliff was from Trinity. Hank is the board chair at First Church."

"You know I'm bad with names," said Frank with a smile. "I can't keep all these people straight."

"But you're right," said Kendall, moving on. "Hank was obsessed with numbers. But then that didn't jive with what I was hearing when I met with the board so I asked him about it."

"Let me get this straight," interrupted Frank. "You called the board chair out on something he'd said at your interview in the middle of another interview? That takes guts, Kendall!"

"I know! I was hesitant, but then I kept thinking about how Jake said it was important to dig into the red flags and I decided to go for it. I'm so glad I did because when I asked Hank about it, he explained that it was really about their philosophy of youth ministry. He wants to see numerical growth because that would indicate an investment in adult leaders, which"—Kendall paused excitedly—"is actually something I'm really good at."

"Wow. So, if you get both offers, you want to take First Church?"

"I don't know." Kendall sighed.

"What do you mean? You just told me all the reasons why you'd be a better fit at First Church!"

"I know," moaned Kendall. "But I'm starting to think the real choice isn't between First Church and Trinity. It's between First Church and staying at Grace. I also know you're pulling for Trinity. I don't want to discount that."

"Again, I appreciate that," said Frank. "But based on what you've said tonight, I think I might agree with you."

"I'm also still really worried that I'm going to screw this decision up. What if we do the wrong thing?"

"We might. But I'm confident that if we do, God will still use you in powerful ways in whatever church you end up serving—just as God has used your time at Grace to bear fruit, despite what a jerk Nate is."

"He's not *always* a jerk," Kendall reminded him. "Didn't you just hear me tell you how awesome he was the other day?"

"One day of awesomeness in three years does not make him worthy of some 'boss of the year' award, Kendall," argued Frank. "But seriously, let's not get ahead of ourselves. All we need to do right now is the next right thing."

"The next right thing," agreed Kendall. "That I can do."

"And right now," said Frank, as their server appeared with their food, "our next right thing is eating these delicious steaks."

"Agreed," laughed Kendall.

■ ■ ■

MONDAY, MAY 11: A DAY OF WAITING

Kendall woke up, wondering if she'd hear from First Church and Trinity, one way or the other.

She worked a full day and waited.

She heard nothing.

■ ■ ■

TUESDAY, MAY 12: ANOTHER DAY OF WAITING

Kendall woke up, wondering if *this* would be the day she'd hear from First Church and Trinity.

She worked a full day and waited.

She heard nothing.

■ ■ ■

WEDNESDAY, MAY 13 AND THURSDAY, MAY 14: TWO MORE DAYS OF WAITING

Kendall woke up on Wednesday, confident *this* would be the day she'd hear from First Church and Trinity.

She struggled to stay present during The Lighthouse's gathering.

By the end of the day, she'd still heard nothing.

Thursday was the same.

■ ■ ■

FRIDAY, MAY 15: STILL ANOTHER DAY OF WAITING

Friday morning, Kendall woke up, sure she'd hear something from First Church or Trinity, especially since she'd heard nothing on Thursday.

She headed to her prayer chair and opened her Bible to Exodus, where the Israelites were now roaming around the wilderness. At this point, she wasn't sure how long they'd been there. Year one or forty? It all felt the same. Just like this relentless waiting did.

She, too, felt like she was roaming aimlessly around the wilderness, perhaps being punished for having dared to think about leaving Nate and Grace in the first place.

■ ■ ■

MONDAY, MAY 18: MORE WAITING

Frank leaned over the breakfast nook expectantly, looking at Kendall as she chugged her morning Pepsi.

"Maybe this will be the day," he said encouragingly.

"I'm not sure how much longer I can wait!"

"The waiting is hard," agreed Frank. "Let's imagine you get the job at First Church. Would you want to leave Springfield and actually move to Capitol City?"

"Good distraction," replied Kendall playfully. "I've been thinking about that. Technically, it's commutable. In some ways, it seems easier to stay here and do that."

"Easier, yes," agreed Frank. "But I'm not sure it'd be better."

"What do you mean?"

"Well, first of all, I think you're going to go crazy driving that much every day. But more importantly, I think it'd be too easy for you to stay enmeshed in the lives of your teens here if we don't move. Just think about Caden. If we still lived here, I could absolutely see you agreeing to disciple her even after we leave Grace."

"There's a chance I've had that exact thought," said Kendall with a grin.

"I know!" exclaimed Frank. "But you and I both know that would not actually be good. As much as it might fulfill you to continue being part of Caden's faith journey, it wouldn't actually be good for her *or* for Grace. They've got to be able to move into a new post-Kendall reality. That'll be hard for them if you're still lurking in the shadows."

Kendall sighed. "That's certainly not what I wanted to hear but you're probably right. Moving would give us a clean break. But you love it here. When we first started talking, you didn't seem all that open to moving. Has that changed?"

"I wasn't," said Frank. "I do love it here but I'm confident I could love Capitol City too. Plus, interest rates are *so* low right now. It's a great time to buy a house!"

"You've been looking at houses already, haven't you?" Kendall gave Frank a knowing look.

"Maybe," responded Frank sheepishly as he dug out his phone and handed it to Kendall. "There's a chance I may have found our dream house."

Kendall scrolled through the pictures on Frank's phone.

"Well," laughed Kendall. "I can see why this is *your* dream house. It comes with a huge yard perfect for gardening *and* a three-car garage. But you know we only have one car, right?"

"I know," admitted Frank. "But someday we might have three!"

"Oh, but here it is." Kendall laughed again, pointing to a picture of a custom workshop in the basement. "This is why you actually want this house, isn't it?"

"It is," confessed Frank. "Just think about all the awesome things I could make for you in a workshop like that!"

"If this would make you excited to move, I don't think you need to keep selling me on it, Frank. But I do think we should sit with this for a few days and see how it feels then," suggested Kendall. "After all, I don't actually have a job offer yet so it might be a moot point."

"Think I should call Jo and Aaron?" Kendall asked Frank after waiting a beat.

"And say what?" Frank bantered.

"I don't know… That they need to decide?!"

"Do you really think that would be helpful?"

"I know it wouldn't," replied Kendall. "But it might make me feel better."

"You can do this, babe," encouraged Frank.

"I know," said Kendall.

Still, when she hadn't heard from either First Church or Trinity by the end of the day, Kendall thought she might rip out her hair.

■ ■ ■

TUESDAY, MAY 19: THE FIRST CALL

As her meeting at Grace came to a close, Kendall heard her phone vibrate. She looked discreetly and saw that it was Aaron. She apologized to her colleagues and said, "I've got to take this" before running out of the room and up to her office.

"This is Kendall," she said as she quickly locked the door.

"Kendall," said Aaron. "I've got what I hope will be some good news for you. You wowed our search committee and we couldn't be happier to offer you the position of youth pastor here at Trinity."

"That's fantastic!" said Kendall, although she wasn't quite as enthused as she hoped she sounded.

"Let me tell you about what we can offer you." Aaron described a very generous salary package, one that was significantly more than Kendall made at Grace. It also came with an additional week's vacation as well as a week for continuing ed and a generous travel allowance to support it.

Kendall had a startling thought. "What's the youth ministry's budget, Aaron?" she asked. "I can't believe I didn't think to ask you about it sooner."

"I'll have to check with our finance guy and get back to you on that one," said Aaron honestly. "Do you have any other questions for me?"

"Not right now," replied Kendall. "I'd like to talk about this with my husband, Frank, and think and pray about it for a bit. Can I contact you with any questions that might come up as I do that?"

"Absolutely," replied Aaron. "And Kendall, we want you to know that it would be a real pleasure to have you join our team."

"Thanks, Aaron. I'm grateful for this opportunity. I'll talk to you soon."

Kendall hung up the phone and collapsed into tears on her couch, surprised by how emotional she felt:

Relief at actually having a job offer in hand.
Gratitude at it being a good one.
Wonder at what ministry might be like at Trinity.
Grief over the possibility of leaving Grace.
And fear that she'd choose wrong.

She called Frank.

"I got the job," she said, not wanting to mince words.

"Which one?"

"The one at Trinity with Aaron. The offer's good," she said, filling Frank in on all the details.

Frank whistled. "How does that offer make you feel?"

"Pretty damn good," Kendall replied honestly.

"Congrats!" said Frank. "So how much are you freaking out?"

"You know me too well. A lot."

"Remember," cautioned Frank, "the next right thing. That's all that we have to figure out."

"Thanks for being my anchor," replied Kendall, before hanging up the phone. She wondered how on earth she'd concentrate the rest of the day.

WEDNESDAY, MAY 20: ANOTHER DAY OF WAITING

Kendall convinced herself that since Trinity called yesterday, First Church would call today.

They didn't.

■ ■ ■

THURSDAY, MAY 21: A BREAKDOWN

When Thursday evening came and Kendall still hadn't heard from First Church, she knew a breakdown was in order. She stormed into Frank's office, not bothering to knock.

"No one is ever going to hire me!" she burst out.

"Don't you think you're being a bit melodramatic?" he asked. "I'm pretty sure Grace hired you. And the two other churches before that. And you just got a job offer from Trinity. A pretty good one, if I recall correctly. What on earth are you talking about?"

"You know exactly what I mean," retorted Kendall. "First Church is never going to hire me. It's the job I want and so of course, I'm not going to get it."

Frank laughed. "If First Church is where God wants you, you'll get the job. But back up here a second. I know we did some initial dreaming about moving if you got the job there, but last I heard, you were still feeling pretty conflicted over whether or not you even want to leave Grace. Since when is First Church the job you really want?"

"Since forever." Kendall exhaled. "I mean, not really. But lately, I've felt such peace about First Church, in a way that I haven't felt about staying at Grace or going to Trinity. Trinity still seems like it would be easier in a lot of ways… But I don't know. I just feel like I'm being called to First Church."

"And you no longer feel like you're being called to Grace?" asked Frank.

"That's not it either," said Kendall honestly. "That's what makes this whole thing so hard. Some days I do, some days I don't. How do I know if it's God's calling me someplace or if my own feelings are?"

"Maybe the two aren't as different as you'd like them to be," suggested Frank. "And, I might add, for someone who doesn't like church platitudes very much, you sure are using them freely. Maybe today will be the day you hear from First Church. Maybe it won't. Don't catastrophize anything, Kendall. You don't know that you haven't gotten this job. And in the meantime, you still have a job to do here at Grace."

"I guess you're right," said Kendall reluctantly. "But waiting is so hard."

"It is," agreed Frank, as he guided Kendall downstairs to the dinner table.

During dinner, Kendall's phone rang. She and Frank both jumped, wondering if this was the moment they'd been waiting for.

Kendall checked the screen and saw that it was Aaron.

"Hi Aaron!" she said, trying to muster up an enthusiasm she didn't feel. "How are you?"

"Great," he replied. "I'm calling for two reasons. First, I wanted to get back to you with regard to your question about the youth ministry's budget. Unfortunately, I was rather surprised by what I found. Right now, our youth ministry's budget is only $2,000, and it looks like it's earmarked for summer camp."

Convinced she must have heard Aaron wrong, Kendall clarified. "You mean there's not really a youth ministry budget for anything other than camp?"

Out of the corner of her eye, Kendall saw Frank do a facepalm. Had she not still been on the phone she might have done the same. Instead, she waited to hear Aaron's answer, hoping she'd misunderstood.

"Well, yes," stuttered Aaron. "I guess that's what I'm saying. I did, however, want to assure you that this is one of those things we'll figure out once you get here. I'm sure we can find a little bit of money for you to get going."

"How can you be sure?" interrupted Kendall, knowing a red flag when she saw one.

"Well, I control the board and I'll let them know you need some money," replied Aaron.

"Control the board? What do you mean you control the board?"

"Well, I don't mean control the board, exactly," said Aaron, starting to get defensive.

"But that's what you just said," said Kendall, refusing to back down, already thinking about how differently Jo led.

"What I meant is that I sit on the board and I know how important a budget is to a youth ministry. You have my word. I'll make sure you have the money you need to begin."

"Thanks, Aaron," replied Kendall, not quite sure if she really believed what he was saying. Like the preaching issue, this just felt like a way to placate her rather than deal with something potentially difficult now. "You said there were two reasons you called. What was the other?"

"I just wanted to see if you had any other questions for me," he said.

Kendall thought for a second, knowing this was her moment to ask about the apartments and the locked doors.

"I do," said Kendall, trying to disguise her uncertainty. "When I interviewed at Trinity, I couldn't help but notice the apartments across the street from you, like we talked about briefly. What can you tell me about the people who live there?"

"What do you mean?" Kendall couldn't decide if Aaron was being genuinely ignorant or purposefully belligerent.

Uncertain what to make of Aaron's question, Kendall decided she was just going to have to ask him explicitly. "Are the people who live in those apartments white?"

Kendall's question was met with silence, which she knew from experience Aaron would fill if she said nothing.

So, she waited.

"Well," Aaron said, sounding as if he'd been caught off-guard. "That was certainly direct! No, most of the people who live there aren't white. There are a lot of Mexicans who live there as well as a few black people."

"What kind of outreach do you do there?" asked Kendall, curious as to how Aaron would respond.

"Outreach?" questioned Aaron. "You mean like evangelism?"

"Possibly," said Kendall. "The apartments looked pretty rundown, though, so I was also wondering if Trinity ever served that community."

"Oh," replied Aaron. "No, I can't say that we have. For the most part, *those* people just stick to themselves. They don't ever really cross the street and come to us…unless it's to ask for money, which, it's our church's policy not to give out. You just never know how people like that might spend it. I mean, we've got to be good stewards of the money God's entrusted us with, right? Plus, we can't have *those* people hanging around here. That would make our folks feel pretty unsafe."

Kendall groaned inwardly, fighting back tears.

"Are those apartments why your doors are locked all the time?"

"Well," said Aaron awkwardly. "I wouldn't say that exactly. In this day and age, you just can't be too careful. We don't want to be the next church that makes the news because it's been the scene of a mass shooting."

Aaron's words left Kendall speechless.

"You still there, Kendall?" asked Aaron.

"I am," replied Kendall.

"You got kind of quiet on me!" said Aaron, trying to make light of the situation.

"Just trying to process everything you just said," replied Kendall honestly.

"Okay," said Aaron hesitantly. "Anything else I can help you with today?"

"I don't think so," said Kendall.

"Do you have a sense of where you are in this discernment process?" prodded Aaron.

"I think I'm getting a lot closer," said Kendall, knowing this phone call had pretty much cemented her decision.

"Think you can let us know your decision by next week?"

"I do," replied Kendall, feeling confident she'd be able to cross Trinity off her list of possibilities after talking over this conversation with Frank. Before she could say anything she might regret later, Kendall decided she better hang up. "Thanks again for calling, Aaron. We'll talk soon."

"All right," said Aaron. "Have a great night."

As soon as she hung up the phone, Frank said, "That didn't sound great."

"It wasn't. I'm pretty sure Aaron all but admitted that they lock the doors of their church because Mexicans and black people live in the apartment buildings across the street and they're afraid they'll get shot if they leave the building open."

"What?!" cried Frank. "He did not just say that. Did he?"

"I mean, not exactly. But he pretty much implied it."

She recounted the entire phone call to Frank, who ultimately agreed with her assessment.

"And they don't have much of a budget."

"What?" asked Frank. "Isn't this the church with the awesome youth room? How can they *not* have a budget? That doesn't even make sense."

"I agree," admitted Kendall. "It doesn't make sense to me either. It also seemed to surprise Aaron, which is also pretty alarming to me. Shouldn't a senior pastor have a handle on the church's finances?"

"You'd think so, wouldn't you," replied Frank. "It sounds like this decision just got easier, though."

"It did," said Kendall. "I can't work for a church that doesn't value *all* people, that doesn't see black and brown people as being created in God's image, too."

"No, you can't, babe," agreed Frank. "That's not who you are."

"But what about you?" asked Kendall. "You liked Trinity."

"No," corrected Frank. "I liked what I thought I knew about Trinity. I liked that it reminded me of home. I don't like that this is their attitude toward people *or* money."

"So, I guess I'm staying at Grace, then," said Kendall, somewhat sadly.

"What?" questioned Frank. "What made you decide that?"

"It's my only option!"

"You don't know that," assured Frank. "You might still get an offer from First Church."

"I guess so," agreed Kendall, although she certainly didn't feel as confident as Frank seemed to be.

"I know so," replied Frank, wrapping Kendall in a big bear hug. "For now, though, let's just go watch more *Parks and Rec.*"

"Yes, please!" agreed Kendall, ready to be immersed into the fictional world of Leslie Knope. It somehow seemed so much more palatable than her current world.

■ ■ ■

FRIDAY, MAY 22:
THE SECOND CALL AND A NEW DEVELOPMENT

"Today's gonna be the day," Frank told Kendall at breakfast.

"That's what you've been saying for the last week," grinned Kendall. "They're never going to call."

Kendall and Frank bantered back and forth before Kendall left to go grocery shopping. On the way to the store, the phone rang. It was Jo.

Taking a calming breath, Kendall braced herself for the bad news she knew was coming.

"Hello, this is Kendall," she said, more calmly than she actually felt.

"Kendall, this is Jo. I apologize it's taken longer than we expected to get back to you. Bob and I agreed I should be the one to call."

Kendall groaned inwardly, more convinced than ever that she was about to get rejected.

"I'm pleased to tell you that after much prayer and discernment, we would be thrilled to have you as our youth pastor here at First Church," said Jo. "On a personal note, I'd love to work with you. I think you'd have much to offer our team, our youth, and perhaps most importantly, our entire church."

Kendall fought back tears, slightly unnerved that she now actually had not one, but two job offers. Convinced there was still bad news, she prepared herself for a less than stellar offer.

Jo continued with all the details of the salary package. The number Jo named was lower than Trinity's, but not by much. It was still higher than what she made at Grace. Like Trinity, First Church's salary package also included an additional week's vacation, five sick days, and a week off for continuing ed along with a generous allowance to support it.

After Jo finished sharing the details of the salary package, she asked Kendall what questions she had. Kendall felt a bit of déjà vu. "I can't believe I didn't ask you this earlier, but what's your youth ministry's budget?"

Jo laughed. "As a matter of fact, that's what delayed our response. We knew we wanted to hire you, but we wanted to make sure we could resource you in a way that reflects how much our congregation values youth ministry. So right after you met with the board, they met for an emergency meeting to suggest approving a new youth ministry budget. Because that budget is radically different than what we've had in the past, our congregation had to ratify it as well, which they did on Wednesday. Your youth ministry budget would be 10% of our congregation's operating budget."

Jo walked her through the actual numbers, which made Kendall's eyes nearly pop out of her head. It was far more than she had at Grace and far more than she'd ever imagined having for a youth ministry budget.

"Wow," was all she could think to say.

"I trust that means the budget meets with your approval?" questioned Jo.

"It does," replied Kendall eagerly.

"Do you have any other questions for me?"

"I do," said Kendall, with a slight hesitation. "This is another one of those things that I'm surprised we haven't already talked about but I think we better before we go any further. As you know, Frank and

I live in Springfield, which we really like. Would you expect us to move to Capitol City in order to live in the same community as First Church?"

"I'm glad you brought that up," replied Jo. "Certainly, we'd prefer for you to live here. It would make things a lot easier for us. Plus, we think Capitol City is pretty great, too. But ultimately, Kendall, that's a decision you and Frank need to make. We'd be thrilled for you to make the move. But we'd understand if you want to stay where you are, at least for a while. Does that seem reasonable to you?"

"Very."

"Is there anything else?" asked Jo.

Kendall very nearly said, "When can I start?" but she knew there was a right way to proceed here. Instead she said, "I don't think so. Let me just have the weekend to think and pray through this decision with Frank."

"That sounds great, Kendall. Please feel free to call Bob or me if you think of more questions."

"Will do," replied Kendall. "Thanks so much for the call, Jo. I'll look forward to talking with you soon."

By then, all Kendall wanted to do was go home and tell Frank her news but instead she walked into Kroger to get her groceries.

As soon as she got home, she ran up to Frank's office. One look at her face and Frank guessed what had happened. Kendall filled him in on the details. "So, I wouldn't be making as much money as I would be at Trinity. Should that sway my response?"

Frank shook his head no. "We both know you'd do this for free. And we both know there's no way you can work for Aaron or serve at Trinity if that's their attitude toward their neighbors. First Church's salary is more than fair. And it's still a great deal more than what you're making now. What impresses me most, though, is how they want to resource the youth ministry with their new budget."

"I know," Kendall said, her eyes filling with tears. "Me too."

"Would they expect us to move?" wondered Frank.

"Nope," Kendall assured him, filling him in on that part of her conversation with Jo.

"Good," admitted Frank. "I'd like to stay where we are for at least a while longer."

"I get that," agreed Kendall.

"So we're going to First Church?" asked Frank.

"I think so," said Kendall. "But I'm scheduled to meet with Jake tomorrow anyway. Let me talk to him first."

"Because that's how we always make decisions," teased Frank. "God, you, me…and Jake."

Kendall headed to her prayer chair, convinced that now more than ever she needed to spend some time with God. Just as she sat down, her phone rang. It was Nate. She was tempted to ignore it, but instead, she picked up.

"Kendall," said Nate, straight to the point as always. "Something has come up. I know you took today off, but would you mind coming into the office? This shouldn't take long."

Curiosity got the better of Kendall's boundaries and she agreed. Knowing that Frank was immersed in his work, she headed out the door wordlessly.

A few minutes later, she arrived at Grace and walked directly toward Nate's office, where she heard another voice, that of their board president, Paul.

Oh crap, Kendall thought. She wondered what kind of trouble she'd gotten herself into now. She felt increasing dread with each step.

When she reached Nate's door, both Paul and Nate rose to greet her with smiles on their faces.

This is so odd, Kendall thought. As she sat down, she silently reminded herself that she had two job offers on the table and that whatever was about to happen wouldn't change that, even if Nate and Paul fired her. Just as her anxiety started to get the better of her, Nate began talking. "I realized the other day that my words of affirmation caught you off guard. I'm sorry about that."

Sorry his words had caught me off guard or sorry he'd never affirmed me? Kendall wondered as she fought to remain silent.

"I meant what I said the other day, Kendall," continued Nate. "You have done exceptional ministry in your time here at Grace. I don't say that often enough, but it's true."

"We want you to know how much you're valued here," said Paul. "I'm a business guy so I know the only real way to show people you're valued is with money."

Now Kendall was really confused.

"We know that you've been underpaid during your entire tenure here," admitted Nate. "So, we'd like to bump you up to a more suitable salary."

Nate showed Kendall a number that was only a bit less than the offer she'd just received from First Church.

Kendall began to weep.

"Umm," replied Paul. "I'm sorry. But I'm really not sure what to make of your tears."

"I'm stunned," admitted Kendall. "I'm also incredibly grateful…and more than a little bit surprised. I also really don't understand. All we ever hear about as a staff is how little money our church has. How can you suddenly afford to give me a raise?"

"Well," said Nate, "I think you know that Jill is a major financial contributor here at Grace. What you might not know is that Caden's parents are also loaded. They've always supported Grace's ministry faithfully and generously. But when they called to tell me how thankful they were for your ministry, they also informed me they'd be doubling their contribution to Grace as a token of appreciation for your ministry's impact on Caden. I knew then that the right thing to do was increase your salary, but I needed to get the board's approval before I could make that commitment."

"We were only too happy to do that," said Paul enthusiastically.

"Again," said Nate, "I want you to know the value you bring to our family of Grace."

"We hope this shows you that," added Paul.

"It does," said Kendall. "Thank you both. I don't know what else to say. But thank you!"

"You're welcome," said Nate. "Now, go home. I'm sorry to have called you in on your day off, but Paul and I couldn't wait to share this news with you."

With that, Nate—always slightly awkward in these moments—ushered Kendall out the door.

Kendall walked home, slightly dazed. When she arrived, she flew up the stairs to share this development with Frank.

"You'll never believe what just happened," she said, filling Frank in.

"Wow!" said Frank. "What a twist! When Jo called today with such a generous offer, I thought for sure we'd be going to First Church. But now I don't know. What are you thinking, babe?"

"I'm thinking I want to go pray." Kendall felt as though she might pass out. "And talk to Jake."

"That sounds like a good plan," agreed Frank with a smile.

"I just can't believe this," muttered Kendall. "I mean, I can. But I can't. Isn't it just like God to surprise me—in the best possible way? I mean, no one else could write this story the way God just did."

"That's for sure," said Frank, with a knowing smile.

■ ■ ■

SATURDAY, MAY 23: MORE ADVICE FROM JAKE

Saturday morning, Kendall headed to The Perk to meet Jake. She grabbed their favorite booth and ordered her usual drink before opening her Bible to Exodus.

She'd spent the last couple of weeks meditating on Exodus 16-17. Each time she read Exodus 16 and the story of God's provision, she was amazed at the ways she felt those verses playing out in her own life, especially in this season of transition, a season which, in so many ways, felt like the wilderness to her.

God had indeed sustained her at Grace, though. Now, it seemed God had provided her with manna: Two job offers, both good, and a significant raise at Grace.

Thanks to her conversation with Aaron, Kendall knew without a doubt that she was going to say no to the job at Trinity. What she didn't know was if she was going to stay at Grace or go to First Church.

As Kendall waited for Jake to arrive, she felt prompted to move onto Exodus 18—the story of Jethro advising Moses. As she read, Kendall couldn't help but see the parallels between Moses's relationship with Jethro and hers with Jake. Not for the first time, she found herself grateful for Jake's ongoing presence and counsel in her life. She wondered how youth workers survived without mentors and felt extraordinarily thankful that she didn't have to find out.

Just then, Jake slid into their booth with a tall black coffee in his hand.

"Well?" he questioned expectantly.

Kendall filled him in on the events of the last week, including her conversation with Nate.

"Wow!" exclaimed Jake. "I'll admit, I did not see that coming."

"I know, right?" agreed Kendall, still in disbelief. "I didn't either!"

"What do you think you're going to do?"

Kendall shared with Jake how much uncertainty she'd been feeling about leaving Grace.

"I'm not surprised," said Jake. "When we prepare to leave a place, sometimes that place starts to look better to us. It's like how after the Israelites left Egypt, they longed to return to slavery."

"But that's the thing," countered Kendall. "I don't feel like I've been enslaved at Grace. Especially now. Nate has all but apologized for the Jill incident. He's said he values me. He's affirmed me. He's even given me a significant raise to prove it."

"That really is something," agreed Jake. "How does the additional money make you feel about working with Nate?"

"Like it's more doable," Kendall replied honestly. "I mean, he's been a different guy the last few weeks. I think he's changed. What if we could really do ministry together?"

"What do you think has changed?" prodded Jake.

"I don't know," Kendall admitted. "That's the part that doesn't make sense to me."

"It doesn't make sense to me, either," Jake said slowly. "That's why I think you need to proceed carefully with Nate. What about Jo? How do you feel about the prospect of working with her?"

"I'd be thrilled to work with her. I like her a lot. I'm intrigued by how she leads. I think I have a lot to learn from her. But I also think she has a lot to learn from me. And I think she really wants me to succeed—so much so that she's intentionally carving out space for me to use my gifts to serve the whole church."

"It sounds like Jo would make for a genuine partner in ministry for you," said Jake thoughtfully. "Do you think you could ever really partner like that with Nate?"

Before Kendall had a chance to answer, Jake interrupted. "Wait. That's the wrong question. Do you think Nate could ever really partner with *you*?"

Kendall sat for a moment, thinking.

"No," she replied a moment later, as her tears began to fall.

"Say more," prompted Jake.

"If Nate could genuinely partner with me," whispered Kendall, "he already would have. I think in the last few weeks, Nate has seen my value. But I think a big part of that is because of Caden's parents and specifically, their financial clout at the church. I'm so blessed by what they did and how Nate decided to use some of that money. It's a gesture unlike anything I've ever seen from him."

"But?"

"But…it's still not partnership, is it?"

"What makes you say that?" Jake said, encouraging her to continue.

"Partnership means us actually doing things together," replied Kendall. "It means us actually working through problems as a team."

Kendall paused, carefully considering something before continuing. "In reality, even Nate's grand gesture reeks of power. Nate and the board decided what to do with the money that Caden's parents gifted them because of me. No one even told me about the money until after they'd decided how best to use it."

Jake nodded, silently encouraging Kendall to go on.

"In contrast, every single thing Jo has said and done indicates a genuine partnership. Even the way she treats her board and other staff reflects that."

Jake waited, sensing that Kendall was reaching an important conclusion.

"It's Jo." Kendall felt surprisingly confident about what she'd just decided. "I want to work with Jo at First Church, as long as Frank's okay with that."

"Why?"

"Because it's my next right thing," said Kendall, with a smile that stretched across her whole face.

"So how are you going to do tell Nate?" asked Jake.

"With an e-mail?" grinned Kendall.

"You know you can't do that, right?"

"I know." Kendall's grin quickly faded. "Honestly, I don't know how to do this. This just got *much* harder. Before, I would have said that there was no love lost between Nate and me. That might still be the case but on the heels of his grand gesture, telling Nate I'm leaving is really gonna suck."

"It will," agreed Jake. "There's no way around that."

"But I still want to end well," said Kendall. "That feels important, especially since I've never left particularly well before."

"As it should," said Jake. "You're a person of integrity. Of course you want to leave well. But what does that actually look like?"

Kendall thought for several minutes. She knew she wanted to leave well but truth be told, she didn't exactly know what that might entail.

Kendall began with what she knew. "I thought I'd call Jo tomorrow to tell her the good news. I'll let Aaron know the bad news right after that. Then, I want to meet with Nate on Monday morning."

"That's important," agreed Jake. "I know we've talked about how sweet this season can be. But now that the offer has come and you've made your decision, you don't want to be a lame duck. Finish your ministry at Grace, take a few weeks off, and then start with enough time to begin well at First Church. Since May is almost over, that doesn't give you much time."

"I know," said Kendall. "It all feels tight to me. When I talk to Nate, do I essentially give him two weeks' notice? Should I give him more than that? What does ending well look like in terms of timing?"

"You may not have a choice in that matter. Once you resign, Nate may tell you what the next few weeks will look like. I hope not, but it's a possibility. Having said that, go into your meeting with him with a plan. Think about your summer calendar at Grace. What's important for you to do? What can your adult leaders take? And what's best for the church to handle independent of you?"

"Our mission trip to Mexico is the second week of June," said Kendall. "It feels important to go on that."

"Why?" challenged Jake. "There's a difference between wanting to go to Mexico for you and genuinely wanting to go because it's the best thing for you to do."

"I appreciate the challenge, Jake," agreed Kendall. "It's important because we've spent the last year planning it. It feels like the culmination of our time together rather than a new beginning. It's the last trip for our seniors and our rising freshmen aren't a part of it so it feels like it might give everyone some closure. My leaders are amazing, and I know they *could* lead this trip without me. But that doesn't mean they *should*. Two weeks out, it doesn't feel right to dump it into their laps."

"Those all sound like good, healthy reasons. I'd affirm it's important for you to be on it. What about the rest of the summer?"

"Everything else feels less dependent on me. I can't think of a single thing I couldn't hand off to my leaders and feel good about. I wonder if I should suggest leaving after the third week of June. That would allow me to take three to four weeks off before starting at First Church but still give me enough time to begin the school year well there."

"That's a really good strategy," encouraged Jake. "Here's the thing, though. As soon as you resign, your ministry no longer belongs to you."

"What do you mean?"

"You have to let go of any dreams you still have for The Lighthouse, your leaders, and your kids," said Jake. "Once you resign, you lose your right to say anything about what happens after you leave. You have to let go of your ownership of this ministry."

"Oh man," said Kendall as her eyes welled up with tears. "That's hard."

"I know," agreed Jake. "That's why I thought I better mention it. Part of what makes you an excellent youth pastor is that you care deeply about your ministry. But you have to let go of this ministry in order to make room—room for the new ministry you're being called to and room for the faith stories your kids will continue writing after you leave."

"You're saying the kids at Grace are no longer mine. Is that it?" questioned Kendall.

"That's it," Jake agreed. "I mean, they've never actually been *your* kids. They're God's kids who were temporarily entrusted to you."

"What does that mean for ongoing communication with them?" Kendall thought again about her conversation with Frank and whether or not she could keep discipling Caden.

"You won't be their youth pastor anymore, Kendall," said Jake gently. "When they reach out to you, you can talk to them. But you can't pastor them. You've got to direct their spiritual questions back to Nate, your leaders, or their parents. When they come to you and complain about your replacement, you've got to defend that person and help them to love whoever comes after you. You've got to let them know they're not being disloyal to you if they like the next youth pastor. You've got to tell them that you *want* them to keep growing in their faith, even without you."

"That's good, Jake," replied Kendall. "Hard, but good. Any other advice for me, oh wise one?"

"As a matter of fact, yes," said Jake. "In some ways, what you're about to experience is a death. It's the loss of a relationship that you've poured into for three years. You'll grieve that. Your kids will grieve that. But you'll grieve it less if you intentionally take time to say the words that need to be said before you leave."

"I can finally let Nate have it then?" questioned Kendall with a smile.

"That's not *exactly* what I had in mind," Jake said, smiling a little back. "Don't say negative things. Those things can't be unsaid. They can't be unheard. So, take time to tell people what they mean to you. Show gratitude. Don't dwell on the things you lacked at Grace or even on the things that led you to leave. Instead, focus on the good. As you leave, share *those* stories."

"Okay," said Kendall.

"Okay?" asked Jake. "That's all you've got?"

"Actually, no," replied Kendall. "What do I say to people that I'm not grateful for? Like Jill? Or maybe even Nate?"

"That's a great question," said Jake. "Don't lie. Don't tell Nate it's been a privilege working for him when it hasn't. But look hard. Think of all the times you defended Nate to Frank and me. Tell him those things."

"Even that won't necessarily be easy," acknowledged Kendall. "Thanks for everything, Jake. You know I'll need more advice soon, right?"

"Happy to give it, Kendall. In the meantime, you and Frank are in my prayers. Actually, Nate and Grace are too. This week will also be hard on them. That's not your fault, nor is it your problem. But it is reality. So, I will hold you all in prayer. Let me know how it goes."

"Will do," said Kendall, rising to give Jake a hug.

She headed home to talk to Frank, who was waiting for her in the kitchen. "Should we hash this out?" he asked.

"Yep," said Kendall.

"Do you know what you want to do?" asked Frank.

"Yep," said Kendall. "Do you?"

"Yep," replied Frank. "Should we do what we always do?"

"Absolutely." Kendall smiled.

She slid a small piece of paper and a pen across the island to Frank before grabbing one for herself. They each wrote down what they thought they should do. Then they traded slips of paper, counted to three, and opened them.

"First Church," they said in unison.

"Oh, thank God," said Kendall, completely and utterly relieved. "I was so worried you were going to write down Grace. I know you don't want to leave Andy and Pete."

"I don't," replied Frank. "But I want what's best for you. And it's not Grace."

"Even with the extra salary?"

"Even then," Frank assured Kendall. "I mean, it was an incredible gesture, the likes of which I never thought I'd see from Nate, but it's still not enough. Even though more money is nice, that's not what you need."

"And what exactly do you think I need?" asked Kendall with a smile, sensing that Frank had reached the same conclusion she had with Jake.

"Partnership," said Frank with a grin. "And you'll have that with Jo."

"Yes," agreed Kendall, as happy tears rolled down her face. "I believe I will."

■ ■ ■

MONDAY, MAY 25: TELLING NATE

When Kendall awoke Monday morning, she felt sure she was going to vomit. That's how nervous she was about telling Nate.

Not for the first time, she second-guessed her decision to leave Grace. In so many ways, it would be easier to stay, especially after Nate's grand gesture.

Then she thought about her conversation with Jo last night. Jo's excitement over her "yes" was palpable. It had made saying "no" to Aaron fairly painless, especially when Aaron reacted with shock, seemingly surprised that anyone would turn him down.

After a quick breakfast with Frank, Kendall slowly walked to Grace. She prayed for the words to say. She kept thinking about what Jake had told her. "Be grateful," she reminded herself. Then she mentally catalogued the things she could honestly be grateful for during her time at Grace:

- An incredible team of adult leaders, including Natalie, Pete, and Andy
- Amazing students, like Caden and Jonathan
- Parents, like Caden's, who had given her a chance to help form the faith of their kids
- The opportunity to figure out who she was as a youth pastor
- Relationships she knew would continue even after she left
- The chance to implement a missions strategy within the youth ministry

- The way things had gotten better with Nate over the last few weeks
- Nate's recognition of her value
- And so much more.

Her heart felt full as she entered Grace, dropped her stuff on her desk, and headed to Nate's office. She sat down and began, knowing that she and Nate had never been much for small talk.

"There's no easy way to say this, Nate," she said. "I'm leaving. I've accepted a job offer at First Church in Capitol City."

"You're what?" Nate asked incredulously.

"I'm leaving, Nate," Kendall repeated, unsure how to continue.

"Why?" asked Nate. "We just gave you a pretty substantial raise!"

Kendall couldn't decide whether or not Nate actually wanted to know the answer to his question. Deciding to take him at face value, she responded graciously, using typical Christianese. "It's not about the money, Nate. This isn't where God is calling me any longer."

Even though it would be fair—and even pastoral—for Nate to ask her more, she hoped he wouldn't.

Thankfully, he let her answer be.

"When?" he asked.

"That's one of the things I'd like us to talk about," she said. "I'm going to start at First Church on August 1 so ideally, I'd like to end my ministry here no later than July 1."

"Do you still want to go to Mexico?" asked Nate, catching Kendall a bit off guard. Up to this point, she hadn't been sure the mission trip was even on his radar.

She replied that she did and explained all her reasons why.

"That makes sense to me," said Nate. "Are there other things you want to finish before leaving?"

"Not necessarily, although I want to hand things off as much as possible, while also giving you the space to begin searching for my replacement."

Nate grabbed his calendar. "Let's do this," he suggested. "Lead the Mexico trip. Then come back and wrap things up here. We'll celebrate and honor you on the fourth Sunday of June, which will also be your last day. I know that's a little earlier than you suggested but is that okay? My experience has been that once someone resigns, there's no need to prolong the process. That's not healthy for anyone."

Kendall nodded in agreement.

Nate continued. "Do you have any suggestions for how you'd like to tell people your news?"

"I wrote a resignation letter."

Kendall handed Nate the letter she'd carefully penned the night before. It was short but eloquent, sharing her plans to leave and expressing her gratitude to the congregation for her time there.

"This is well done, Kendall," said Nate after reading it. "When would you like this to go out? Do you want families to know about your plans before you leave for Mexico?"

"I do," replied Kendall emphatically. "I've thought a lot about that. It will be hard, but I think that will give me closure with the kids. Plus, it would feel dishonest to me if they didn't know, especially given how quickly I'll be gone after we return."

"That makes sense," said Nate, leaving Kendall slightly amazed by his agreement. "Then here's my suggestion. Why don't you tell everyone at tomorrow's staff meeting? Once the staff knows, our office team can get your letter out. That will give you time to tell the kids on Wednesday, during your last meeting of the year. You can have an e-mail ready to go out to the parents during your meeting so that they'll know by the time their teens gets home. Then, we'll announce it in worship on Sunday. Does that sound reasonable?"

"Yes…The only thing I'm unsure about is telling the kids on Wednesday. I've got a lesson planned that I still want to do. I don't want Wednesday to just be about me."

Nate thought for a moment. "Why don't you tell your teens at the *end* of your time together that night? Then you can spend Thursday following up with kids who need more one-on-one care."

"That's actually a good idea," said Kendall, no longer trying to hide her surprise at how well this was going. "There is one thing, though. I don't want my adult leaders finding out on Wednesday with the kids or through a generic letter mailed to everyone. Would it be okay with you if I connected with them between now and then? If they know before Wednesday night, they can be prepared to care for our teens once they find out the news. That's going to be important."

"I agree," said Nate. "I'm going to want to spend some time with your leaders, too, as we begin thinking about what's next for our youth ministry here. You've done an extraordinary job building a team of adult leaders, Kendall. I want to make sure they're part of whatever comes next."

"Thanks," replied Kendall, astounded that Nate had even noticed the team she'd built. "I'm sure my leaders will appreciate having input into what happens next. I'll let them know you'll be in touch."

"That sounds good, Kendall. Let's schedule some time together later this week. I'd like for you to tell me about how you see our youth ministry and how you'd move forward if you were still going to be here this fall."

"I'd be happy to do that," replied Kendall, shocked Nate was asking her.

"I know we haven't always done well together," said Nate. "But Kendall, I want you to know that I'm deeply grateful for what you've given to Grace during the time you've been here."

"And I'm deeply grateful for the opportunity I've had to be here," said Kendall, doing the best she could to be authentic but gracious.

"Is that all?" asked Nate, making it clear that their conversation was done.

"It is," said Kendall.

When she got back to her office, she sent a flurry of e-mails to her adult leaders, asking to meet with them one-on-one before Wednesday's final youth gathering. As much as she was dreading these conversations, she knew they were an important part of leaving well.

That night when she got home, she found the house empty.

Happy to be alone, Kendall sat down in her prayer chair and flipped open her Bible. Her bookmark was still in Exodus 16, the manna chapter. As she went to move her bookmark, she glanced down. Her eyes lingered on verse 3:

"The Israelites said to them, 'If only we had died by the hand of the Lord in the land of Egypt, when we sat by the fleshpots and ate our fill of bread; for you have brought us out into this wilderness to kill this whole assembly with hunger.'"

Every other time she'd read this verse, it had struck Kendall as absurd. While in Egypt, the Israelites had longed for their freedom. Yet, shortly after finding their freedom, all they wanted was to return to the familiarity of Egypt. She'd never understood how people who were finally free could long for oppression and captivity.

Tonight she saw this verse differently. Hours after resigning, she felt herself longing for Egypt, wondering if she'd made a colossal mistake in leaving Grace. Things had gone so well with Nate. She wondered if maybe she hadn't given him the chance he really deserved.

By the time Frank walked in, Kendall was curled up in a ball, tears streaming down her face.

"That bad?" asked Frank as he came up behind her, gently putting his hand on her shoulder.

"Not at all," sniffed Kendall. "It was actually really good."

"Good?" asked Frank, his confusion evident as he came around so that he could see her. "Then why are you crying?"

"Because I made a mistake!" cried Kendall. "I want to go back to Egypt and I haven't even really left!"

"What are you talking about?" wondered Frank, clearly confused.

"The Israelites," responded Kendall, frustrated that Frank was not understanding what she was talking about. "After they had their freedom, they just wanted to go back to Egypt. I think that might be my story. For months, I've wanted a new job and now that I finally have one, I think maybe I'm doing the wrong thing."

"The wrong thing?"

Kendall recapped how well her conversation with Nate had gone that morning. "I've made him the villain in my story. I'm not sure he always deserved it."

"Oh, he deserved it!" laughed Frank. "Let me recap the ways he's made your life miserable the last few months…let alone years."

Kendall listened before responding, "But he's such a good preacher!"

"As we've clearly seen, that's not enough. As much as you might like for it to be, that's never been enough. And besides, remember what it was like to watch First Church's online service yesterday? Jo's a pretty good preacher, too. Based on what you said, I think she might also be a good pastor. Maybe she'll even pastor you in a way that Nate never has."

"Thanks, Frank," said Kendall. "I think you're going to need to keep reminding me why I'm leaving Grace. Right now, the thought just makes me sad."

"That's okay," said Frank. "You're allowed to be sad. This is a real loss. But there's something good on the other side. Just think about the Israelites. They wandered around for forty years before finally reaching the promised land. Maybe First Church is your promised land."

"Maybe," agreed Kendall, holding onto hope that it would be, even as she allowed herself to sit with her sadness in this moment.

■ ■ ■

WEDNESDAY, MAY 27: THE DREADED TELLING

By mid-afternoon on Wednesday, Kendall was already exhausted.

She'd spent the day meeting one-on-one with her trusted adult leaders, ensuring that none of them would be caught off guard by tonight's announcements. The conversations were hard but honest. She shared she was leaving, expressed her gratitude for their ministry together, and answered their questions. She made it her goal to affirm each person she spoke to. She was careful to answer questions honestly, while not saying anything she'd regret later. She didn't want to overshare, nor did she want to say anything that might ruin someone else's relationship with Nate or Grace. She was well aware that even though she was leaving, Grace would continue to be her leaders' church.

Knowing she needed a break, Kendall went home before her last youth gathering. Although she wanted to curl up in bed and sleep, she instead sat in her prayer chair and flipped open her Bible to Exodus. She hoped she'd be able to find some good news in the midst of the wilderness.

Kendall read Exodus 19, the story of the Israelites being consecrated. She was struck by verse 17, when Moses brought the people out of the camp to meet God.

Yet again, this was a verse she'd read many times—but never before had it jumped out to her. Now, as she read it, she prayed that tonight she'd lead her teens to meet God, as she hoped they had every Wednesday of the years she'd been there.

After finishing her quiet time, Kendall looked at her watch and realized she needed to get back to Grace. Once there, she set up the youth room for their gathering. As always, she wandered around, silently praying for the teens who'd soon sit in the chairs. Today, she prayed especially for the right words to use when telling them her news. She prayed people would receive it well and that she and her leaders would have the grace and wisdom to respond appropriately.

After finishing her youth room prep, Kendall returned to her office, where she read through the e-mail she'd composed earlier to her high school families. She wanted to be sure she got this right.

Dear High School Families—

I wanted to share some important news with you that I also shared with our teens tonight at The Lighthouse.

After much discernment and prayer, I have accepted a call to be the Youth Pastor at First Church in Capitol City, effective August 1. This decision was not easy but Frank and I are confident that it is right for us.

I will still be leading our trip to Mexico next week. Upon returning, I will wrap up my ministry here before ending my time with Grace on June 28.

It has been a privilege to serve you these last three years. You have taught me so much, and I am thankful for the role you each have played in my life.

Grateful—
Kendall

Satisfied that her e-mail said what it needed to, Kendall set it to send at 7:15 p.m. that night, hoping most parents would read it by the time they picked up their kids.

After that, Kendall returned to the youth room, determined to make the most of her last night with her kids. The night passed in a blur, which is how Kendall knew the Spirit was at work. It was always like that for her: When she couldn't remember the details of what happened during youth group, she could tell the Holy Spirit had been particularly active.

Before she knew it, it was time for the moment she'd been dreading since her conversation with Nate on Monday. She stood up and faced her kids. "I've got something important to tell you," began Kendall. "On Monday, I gave my resignation to Nate. As of June 28, I will no longer be your youth pastor. I've accepted another position at First Church in Capitol City. This wasn't an easy decision. The hardest thing about this is leaving you. You guys have meant so much to me these last three years. I will miss each of you," Kendall's voice trailed off as she frantically tried to quell her tears. Unsure what else to say, she was relieved to see Natalie jump on stage and wrap her arm around her in an awkward side hug.

"I know Kendall is happy to answer your questions," interjected Natalie. "But before we do that, let's close tonight in prayer."

For the next few minutes, Kendall's leaders prayed for her while her kids stood, some of them crying and clinging to one another, unsure what to say. As soon as Natalie said amen, they swarmed to the front of the room.

Panicked, Jonathan raced toward Kendall. "What about Mexico?" he asked worriedly.

"Oh my gosh!" shouted Kendall. "I almost forgot! I'm still going to Mexico but that'll be my last real thing here. I'll be around for a bit after that, and then we'll say our official goodbyes on Sunday, June 28."

Kendall's kids broke into a relieved cheer.

■ ■ ■

SATURDAY, JUNE 13: A TEARFUL LAST DAY IN MEXICO

The Lighthouse's mission trip was always a highlight for those who participated. This year, Kendall found herself savoring every part of the time with her kids. While the work was meaningful, the team's debriefs were exceptionally good.

Rather than lead everything herself, she'd asked each of her leaders to be in charge of a debrief. Kendall had been impressed (and a little surprised) with how well her leaders had led. She felt confident that these processing times would continue to be central to Grace's mission trips from here on out.

Having her leaders debrief also freed Kendall to spend even more time with her teens. One by one, she'd hung out individually with each teen on the team. Because her relationship with every person in her ministry looked different, the conversations were all different. One thing united them: They were hard but holy.

By Saturday, she'd met with everyone except Caden. In so many ways, Kendall was most sad to be leaving Caden. Odd, because she wasn't a senior who'd known Kendall the longest. She wasn't a student leader who Kendall had spent the most time with. She was simply a student who Kendall felt connected to and had shepherded through the recent growth spurt in her faith. More than anyone else, Kendall struggled with feeling like she was abandoning Caden. Although she'd worked hard not to create a ministry dependent on herself, she worried Caden's faith would deteriorate after her departure.

This was what was going through her mind on Saturday afternoon, when Kendall grabbed two bottles of Coke and headed out to the porch looking for Caden. She found her surrounded by three other girls from The Lighthouse whom she'd grown close to during the trip. Kendall was encouraged to see the way these relationships were blossoming.

She debated going back inside when Caden looked up and waved her over. "Got a minute to talk, Caden?" asked Kendall, offering her one of the Cokes.

"Absolutely," replied Caden, promising her friends she'd be back shortly.

"Let's go to the roof," suggested Kendall, motioning to the staircase their team had found earlier. It led to a flat roof, from which you could see the Mexican countryside. Overlooking their surroundings, they began talking about the week. Since this was Caden's first mission trip, Kendall wanted to help her process it.

"It's been so good," Caden said.

"What's been good about it?"

"Everything," replied Caden.

"You know I'm not going to let you get away with that, right?" joked Kendall.

Caden grinned. "I've loved getting to know Monica, Rachel, and Lindsey," she said, referencing the three girls she'd just been hanging out with. "Since they don't go to my school, they're not people I really knew before this trip. But I think—or at least I hope—that our friendship is going to last even after we get home."

"I've had a lot of fun seeing your relationship with them form," agreed Kendall. "I knew you guys had a lot in common—even if you didn't know it yourselves. That's why we assigned you to the same bunk room."

"I should have known you did that intentionally." Caden smiled.

"What else has been good for you?" questioned Kendall.

"I've really enjoyed the work," Caden said. "Not the physical work so much. I mean, I don't love mixing concrete. But I've really enjoyed leading VBS. When we prepared for that, I couldn't wrap my head around how we'd communicate with these kids since we don't speak Spanish. But we've made it work. And it's been pretty amazing."

"It has, hasn't it?" agreed Kendall.

"It's also just been so good to be with you, Kendall," said Caden, before promptly bursting into tears.

Kendall felt her own eyes well up, too. "Back at you," she told Caden.

"I'm having such a hard time imagining The Lighthouse without you," Caden admitted.

Kendall nodded, encouraging Caden to continue. "You've meant so much to me and everyone else here. I just don't know if I'm still going to want to come without you. What if the next person changes *everything*?"

Kendall knew she'd reached an important moment. This, too, was an opportunity to disciple Caden. She also knew that what she said would impact not just Caden's willingness to continue going to The Lighthouse but also the girls Caden had become close with. She quickly asked God to give her the right words before continuing. "It's going to be different. There's no way around that. I'm so sorry for that. I'm also sorry that I won't get to continue being part of your faith story in the same way that I am right now. That was honestly the hardest part of this decision for me."

"Really?" asked Caden.

"Really," said Kendall emphatically. "I don't want to leave you guys. But here's what I know. You have great adult leaders—including Natalie—who will still be here after I leave. They care deeply about you and your faith journey. So do your parents, Caden. You are not alone."

Caden nodded and used the back of her hand to wipe away some of her snot. "I hope you're right," she said, not sounding convinced.

"Here's something else I know," continued Kendall. "The Lighthouse needs you. You are a beautiful young woman, inside and out. You ask incredibly good questions. You need to ask them, and your friends also need you to keep asking those questions because they have them, too."

"Then why don't they ever open their mouths and say something?" wondered Caden.

"Because they're not as brave as you are. That's one of the things The Lighthouse needs right now. Brave people like you who are willing to say what needs to be said. You need to keep coming because in the last year, you've become a leader amongst your peers, Caden. That's a gift. And I can't wait to see how you develop that gift. I'm sad I won't have a front-row seat for that, but rest assured, I'll be keeping track of you."

"Really?" asked Caden again.

"Really," assured Kendall. "Even though I won't be your youth pastor anymore and I'll want you to connect to the next one, you can still text me. Tell me how you're doing. Let me know how I can pray for you. Ask me a question every once in a while. I'll still be in your life. That'll just look different. It's okay to grieve that. I know I am."

"You mean you won't be mad at me if I'm not happy you're leaving?" Caden asked with a worried look.

"Are you kidding?" grinned Kendall. "I'd be a little disappointed if you were happy! We've meant a lot to each other this last year. Grief shows that our relationship was and is important. Grief's important in this process. There's no rushing it. You should also know that grief includes other emotions, like anger."

"Truthfully, I have been a little angry at you, Kendall," admitted Caden. "I didn't want to tell you that, but it's true. How can you leave us *now*? Right when I need you?"

"Oh, Caden," replied Kendall. "I don't have a good response to that. My husband, Frank, and I have been praying about this for a long time. We don't completely understand it ourselves, but we feel like God's calling us to First Church."

"That's such a copout," said Caden, her anger showing now.

"What do you mean?" asked Kendall.

"You know I can't argue with God, so it feels like you're saying that as your trump card to silence me."

"That's honestly not my intent, Caden. Since I'm still your youth pastor, I'm going to tell you this: You *can* argue with God. The Psalms are *filled* with people arguing with God. Actually, the whole Bible includes people arguing with God. God is big enough to handle your anger and hurt."

"Really?" asked Caden, a little unsure as to whether she believed this.

"Really," Kendall assured. "I'll admit. I've done a *lot* of arguing with God over this whole leaving thing."

"Then why go?" asked Caden again.

"Because sometimes the things we're being asked to do are hard. Even though this feels hard, Frank and I are confident it's our next right thing."

"Your next right thing?" wondered Caden.

"Our next right thing," replied Kendall. "Frank and I have decided that instead of trying to plan out our whole lives, we're just going to do our next right thing."

"Your next right thing," echoed Caden. "I like that."

"What do you think your next right thing is, Caden?" asked Kendall.

Caden paused, wanting to give the question some thought. After a moment, she replied, "Two things. First, I think it's to study the Psalms. I want to see some of the anger you mentioned myself."

"I love that," replied Kendall, nearly overcome with sorrow that she wouldn't be around to guide Caden through that part of her faith journey. "What's your second next right thing?"

"I think I need to keep going to The Lighthouse," Caden said. "Maybe they really do need me. Maybe I could even be an official student leader someday."

"I hope so!" exclaimed Kendall. "Caden, I'm so proud of you. You are loved. By me and by God."

"That's cheesy," replied Caden, reaching out to Kendall for a hug.

"I know," Kendall said. "But it's true."

Together, they walked back downstairs, where they found dinner ready and waiting.

At the start of dinner, Jonathan led them in a thought-provoking devotion, which once again made Kendall both insanely proud and crazy sad about the prospect of leaving.

As soon as dinner was cleaned up, Natalie gathered everyone, to Kendall's surprise. Although she'd given all their debriefing responsibilities to her adult leaders, she'd intentionally reserved Saturday night to lead herself. It was a Lighthouse tradition to close out mission trips with a candlelight ceremony in which each team member got to say one thing they'd learned on the trip, one thing they were grateful for, and a way they'd seen God move during the week, or share whatever was on their heart. She'd been looking forward to leading the ceremony all week.

Natalie spoke. "Before we start our traditional candlelight ceremony, we wanted to do something for you, Kendall. We know it's been a great week, but we've all been acutely aware of the fact that your time with us is rapidly coming to a close. So, we wanted to honor you. Would you please come here?" Natalie motioned to a chair she'd set up in the middle of a circle of other chairs.

"Here's what we've got planned," said Natalie. "Each member of our team brought you a small gift that represents you. We're each going to give you our gift and then tell you its meaning."

For the next hour, each team member presented Kendall with their gift, thoughtfully explaining why they'd chosen it. In the process, Kendall was affirmed again and again for her ministry at Grace. She wept the entire time, once again wondering why she was leaving. The fruit of her ministry was so evident. *Why throw it all away?* she wondered to herself.

As luck (or God) would have it, the last teen to go was Caden. Caden made her way toward Kendall carrying what looked to be a very used journal. Before she even reached the center, Caden was in tears. So was Kendall.

"You changed my life this year," began Caden. "Our series on the trustworthiness of the Bible really messed me up. In a good way," she added quickly.

"Before then," continued Caden, "I really struggled to read Scripture. Now I love it. You gave me a framework for understanding Scripture that I'd always lacked. But doing that also raised a lot of questions for me. When I first started asking you those questions, I was scared about how you'd respond. I shouldn't have been. You always responded with grace. Instead of answering my questions, you'd raise another one that would send me back to Scripture, looking for more answers. About a month ago, you encouraged me to journal my questions and what I was learning. I took your idea seriously. My gift to you is my journal. Even though I've only been journaling for a short time, this one is nearly full. I want you to see how much you've made me think. Thanks to these questions, my faith has grown more in the last few months than it ever has before."

Caden handed Kendall her journal and gave her a big hug. Kendall could not believe what a gift she'd just been given. To see that Caden had taken her advice so seriously and that that advice had transformed her faith was incredible. To be invited into that sacred, personal journal and allowed to read it was a gift the likes of which Kendall had never been given.

Seeing that Kendall was overcome with emotion, Natalie acted quickly.

"Kendall, you are loved—by us and God," she said, repeating the phrase that Kendall had so often told her kids during the years she'd been at Grace.

"Let's hug it out, everyone," Natalie commanded. The teens descended on Kendall, surrounding her with the biggest, most meaningful group hug she'd ever received.

Just when Kendall feared she was about to be smothered, Natalie interrupted. "I know we still have our candlelight ceremony to do, but we could use a stretch and drink break first. Let's meet back here in fifteen minutes."

The group dispersed, leaving Kendall alone with her leaders.

"Thanks, guys," she said. "This means more to me than you'll ever know. I'm deeply grateful for each and every one of you."

Her leaders nodded, enveloping Kendall in yet another round of hugs. Kendall then headed to her room to compose herself.

The candlelight ceremony lasted hours, way longer than it should have. But her teens and leaders had things to say. Much to Kendall's delight, their comments were focused. They were about faith, God, and what they'd learned in Mexico. She savored every last one of them.

By the time the night concluded, Kendall fell into her bunk bed, completely and utterly exhausted but filled to the brim, overcome with both grief and hopefulness. She recognized that her time at Grace was coming to a good, necessary close. And she felt excited by the prospect of beginning anew at First Church.

■ ■ ■

SUNDAY, JUNE 28: THE CELEBRATION

In her entire time at Grace, Kendall had never dreaded attending worship as much as she did on her last day.

Before heading out the door, Frank gave her a big hug. "It's okay for the people at Grace to see you cry today," he whispered in her ear.

Kendall smiled gratefully. This was part of what she was worried about. She was fearful she'd lose it today, if not in worship, then during the subsequent celebration.

As she slid into her pew with Frank and all the youth group orphans, Kendall smiled, although her heart felt heavy knowing this would be the last time she sat there.

She was pleasantly surprised when Nate lifted up her ministry as a part of his sermon.

After the offering, Nate called her forward for the sending ritual. They'd actually worked together the previous week to craft what this would look like. What they'd written released her from her ministry at Grace and offered a blessing for her future ministry at First Church. Kendall couldn't help but wonder why she and Nate had been able to work so well together on this when they'd failed so colossally at collaboration over the past three years. Nevertheless, what they created was deeply meaningful and important. For everyone to move on, Nate and Kendall agreed that both she and Grace needed the sense of closure they hoped this ritual would bring.

As soon as Nate called her forward, Kendall's tears came. She thought about what Frank had told her earlier and made no effort to hide them. Instead, she wept openly as the people of Grace stretched out their hands in a sign of blessing. Though her vision was clouded by her tears, she forced herself to look around, making eye contact with those she'd grown so fond of.

She noticed Jill lingering in the back of the church, her hands at her side rather than extended out in a blessing. Although she could not feel gratefulness toward Jill, Kendall did feel herself release the resentment she'd been harboring. Kendall realized that none of this was actually Jill's fault...nor was it even Nate's fault. It just was. And God was here, in the midst of the myriad of emotions she was feeling.

As the blessing ended, applause broke out and Nate moved toward Kendall for a hug, which she awkwardly accepted. "Thanks," she whispered in his ear.

"Thank you," Nate replied quietly. Then he turned her around to face the congregation. In a rather stunning pastoral act, he whispered, "Enjoy this moment, Kendall."

After worship ended, everyone moved into the gym for a meal to celebrate Kendall's ministry. The teens roasted her. Her leaders toasted her. And then Nate thanked Kendall.

"Kendall and I have not had the easiest relationship," Nate began. "But I want to publicly say how much I've appreciated her ministry to our teens. As our parents and teens can attest, she loves Jesus deeply and worked hard to ensure that they each formed a real, genuine relationship with Jesus that has transformed their everyday lives."

Looking straight at Kendall, he continued. "Our teens' lives have been transformed by your ministry here and we are deeply grateful for it. We trust that God will continue to use you in powerful ways in the ministry of First Church."

Kendall took a slow breath, inwardly wishing that Nate had been more encouraging and appreciative during her ministry at Grace, wondering once again if leaving was the right decision. Sensing her thoughts, Frank leaned over and whispered, "It's easy to say nice things about someone when they're leaving. It's much harder to do that *all the time*."

Kendall smiled back before standing to offer her own heartfelt thanks to Nate and the people of Grace. The celebration ended with pictures, prayer, and the presentation of a book of notes from Grace. Kendall knew she would treasure it always.

■ ■ ■

MONDAY, JUNE 29 – THURSDAY, JULY 9: DEEPLY-NEEDED REST

Although she'd been religious about taking *all* of her vacation during each of her years at Grace, Kendall had no idea how absolutely exhausted she was until her ministry there concluded.

For the first eleven days after her last day at Grace, all she did was sleep.

And it was good.

Very good.

■ ■ ■

FRIDAY, JULY 10: A CONVERSATION WITH NATALIE

By the end of her second week off, Kendall was starting to go a little stir-crazy. She was relieved when Natalie asked her to meet for a walk on their favorite trail.

They talked nonstop, catching up. As they did, Kendall realized how much she missed Natalie. It was so strange to go from seeing someone all the time to hardly seeing them at all.

As they walked, Kendall debated whether or not to ask Natalie how things were going at church. She'd heard through the grapevine that Natalie was part of the task force Nate had assembled to both hire her replacement and figure out how to keep the youth ministry going in the interim.

Kendall finally worked up her nerve. "How's it going at Grace?"

Natalie sighed. "It's really hard, Kendall." She rattled off a laundry list of decisions they were wrestling with along with a litany of frustrations she and the other committee members had with Nate.

Kendall wanted so badly to chime in. She had thoughts—SO MANY THOUGHTS—about what Natalie could and should do. But she thought about what Jake had told her: Leaving meant she no longer had a stake in this ministry. In order for everyone to move on, she could not continue to guide them, even invisibly, from a distance. She listened empathetically and asked questions, but offered no advice.

When they reached the end of the loop, Kendall and Natalie embraced warmly, each glad to have connected with the other.

As Kendall got in her car, she left encouraged that those relationships she cared most deeply about at Grace would in fact continue—albeit on new ground.

■ ■ ■

FRIDAY, JULY 17: NEW COMMANDMENTS

As stir-crazy as Kendall sometimes felt, she was also acutely aware that soon she would be starting a new youth ministry position and life would get hectic again.

That was on her mind as she opened her Bible to Exodus 20: The Ten Commandments.

Although she could spin these commandments to reflect the understanding that they were God's ten best ways, she'd been dreading getting to this chapter, afraid that it would have nothing to offer her.

As she read, though, Kendall began seeing these commandments in a new light, specifically as they might pertain once she began her new role at First Church.

As she read, she journaled: **TEN COMMANDMENTS FOR YOUTH PASTORS.**

1. You shall have no other gods before God. No pastor, no position, and no parent—regardless of how powerful they are—is your god.

2. You shall not make for yourself an idol. Your job cannot and should not be your idol.

3. You shall not make wrongful use of the name of the Lord your God, no matter how frustrated you get with the kids, their parents, or your new colleagues.

4. Remember the Sabbath day and keep it holy. Your Sabbath is

not and cannot be Sunday. That is a workday for you. But you will rest—at least one full day each week. This will help you remember that there is one Savior and it's not you.

5. Honor the fathers and mothers as well as the other grownups who are significant in the lives of your kids. They're not perfect. They *will* frustrate you. But they're doing the best they can. What's more, they're far more important than you'll ever be. They, not you, are the primary spiritual influencers in the life of their child.

6. You shall not murder, nor shall you even think about murdering, that annoying kid, their equally annoying parent, or your boss.

7. You shall not commit adultery. Frank loves you. He always has. He always will.

8. You shall not steal. That means that you shouldn't even grab a ream of printer paper to bring home. This church is being exceedingly generous with you. Steward their resources well.

9. You shall not bear false witness against anyone in your ministry, even when it might seem inconsequential or might (temporarily) make your life better. When you make a mistake, own it. Apologize when necessary.

10. You shall not covet your neighbor's house, wife, etc. etc. etc. Nor shall you covet another youth pastor's job. Nor shall you wish you're back in Egypt, even when it feels like you're entering the wilderness again. You shall not compare your worst to someone's else's best.

Kendall put down her pen and reviewed her words. *This has legs*, she thought to herself.

Later, as she and Frank sat around their firepit, she showed him what she'd written. He nodded approvingly and said, "Can I add one more?"

"Only one?" Kendall joked.

"For now," smiled Frank. "You shall not be too hard on yourself because bad days will come. And when they do, God will still be your God. God will still be there with you. And so will I."

"Amen," replied Kendall. "Amen."

■ ■ ■

SATURDAY, JULY 18: REACHING FOR THE PROMISED LAND

When Saturday came, Kendall was relieved to reconnect with Jake, something they hadn't done since before she left Grace. She was eager to talk with him about how surprisingly difficult these in-between weeks had been. She'd expected to enjoy them immensely. Instead, she felt stuck, as though she were treading water. She felt restless and untethered. She also felt a growing animosity toward Nate, which surprised her since she'd worked so hard to leave well.

She slid into their normal booth at The Perk, thankful when Jake sat down just a few seconds later. Despite her introverted nature, she was done being alone. Right now, she craved time with people.

Jake took one look at Kendall and said, "This interim time is hard, isn't it?"

"It is," said Kendall, glad that Jake understood. "I was so excited to have the time off. Everyone told me I needed to take it, but I'm starting to feel like I'm going crazy!"

Jake smiled, relating to the feeling. "It's a strange sensation to go from being heavily scheduled with meaningful work to having nothing on your calendar."

"That's exactly it. I know my identity doesn't come from what I do... Or at least I thought I knew that, until I wasn't doing anything. Now I'm not so sure. Maybe my identity is more tied to my work than I'd like to admit."

"Maybe," agreed Jake. "Or maybe it's more difficult than you imagined having so much time to yourself to process your experience at Grace.

Does that sound possible?"

"It does," said Kendall. "Very much so. I was really intentional in leaving Grace. I thought a lot about how to leave well. I did all the right things. Nate was even really kind to me at the end. He finally saw my value. He gave me a significant raise. Even though I shocked him with my resignation, he helped me leave well. He worked so well with me to design a celebration that was really meaningful."

"I'm sensing a 'but,'" prodded Jake.

"But now, almost a month later, I'm feeling angry toward Nate. Resentful, even."

"I was wondering if you'd experience that," replied Jake honestly.

"I don't understand these feelings!" cried Kendall.

"They're hard," said Jake. "I wonder if, despite Nate's grand gesture or perhaps even because of it, you started to let Nate off the hook for some things he's actually responsible for."

"What do you mean?"

"I know you had a tendency to excuse Nate's bad behavior, to let him get away with quite a lot because he was your boss. You respected him in the pulpit, and you wanted to learn from him. Did you find yourself doing that even more than usual toward the end of your time at Grace?"

She reluctantly nodded her head in agreement.

"I wonder if there are still things you need to say to Nate for your own healing. That's part of what this time is for, Kendall. I know you love the church. You don't have to tell me that. But the church—and Grace in particular—wounded you. You need to spend some time processing those hurts and giving yourself permission to name and grieve them."

"That feels like a step backward," muttered Kendall.

"It might feel that way. But it's an important step for you to take if you want to start your new role at First Church in a healthy place."

"But I'm finished at Grace now. How am I supposed to say the things I need to say to Nate? It's not like I can just go back and meet with him."

"Maybe you could," encouraged Jake. "Would that be helpful?"

"Well," said Kendall, "you seem to think it would be."

"Do *you* think it'd be helpful?" prodded Jake.

"I don't know…maybe."

"You could also write him a letter, which you may or may not actually mail to him. What's important is to get the words out, to say what needs to be said. It's not necessarily important for him to hear them."

"Isn't Nate hearing my words necessary for reconciliation?"

"It is," said Jake. "But you're looking for healing, which might not be synonymous with reconciliation. Does that make sense?"

"I think so," replied Kendall honestly.

"Maybe give it a try this week," encouraged Jake. "How are you feeling about First Church?"

Kendall smiled in a way that reached all the way to her eyes. "So good," she said excitedly. "I've had several good conversations with Jo over the last couple of weeks, although I've been really intentional not to start until it's actually August 1."

"That's good," agreed Jake. "I know this in-between time has been hard for you, but I still think it's important to have it."

"Keep telling me that," grinned Kendall. "You know that I've been reading Exodus. I can't help but think that maybe First Church is my promised land. You know, the dream job I've always wanted. It feels so different than Grace, even at the beginning of my time there."

"It definitely makes sense to me that you'd think that," began Jake. "But you need to exercise caution here, Kendall."

"What do you mean?" she asked worriedly.

"I can see why First Church would feel like the promised land to you," began Jake. "And you've exercised a ton of care and thought in this discernment process, so I also really believe it's the right choice. But no church is ever perfect. You just haven't been around Jo and First Church long enough to know its baggage. Remember, Jesus came to heal the sick. And churches are full of imperfect people. If you expect First Church to be perfect, which is what I assume you mean when you equate it with the promised land, then you're setting yourself—and them—up for disappointment. Maybe even for failure."

"Wow," whispered Kendall. "Way to burst my bubble, Jake."

"Better now than once you start at First Church," laughed Jake.

"Seriously, though," continued Kendall. "This will be a good fit for me, right Jake?"

"I know you need assurance," said Jake. "But I can't give you that. Having walked with you through this process, though, I think you made a good decision. I'm confident God will honor that. You'll encounter God in new ways during your ministry at First Church. For now, your only job is to do the next right thing."

Kendall smiled. "That's what Frank keeps telling me."

"I know," said Jake with a grin. "I taught him that."

"Oh man," said Kendall. "I always forget just how far back we go. I'm grateful for you, Jake. Frank is too."

"I know," said Jake seriously. "I'm grateful for you as well. It's such fun to walk this road with you. You know how Jesus always told his disciples they'd do greater things than him? That's how I feel about you."

"Wow," replied Kendall. "I'm not sure I deserve that vote of confidence, but it's sure a nice sentiment."

"I'll keep saying it until you believe it," said Jake.

"I know you will," said Kendall. "And I'm grateful."

The two got up and headed to their cars, promising to talk soon. Kendall had no doubt she'd reach out to Jake as soon as the first crisis hit at First Church. She was grateful to know she could.

■ ■ ■

FRIDAY, JULY 31: THE LETTER TO NATE

After talking with Jake, Kendall found it easier to savor each day of her last week off before beginning her ministry at First Church. Frank even surprised her with three days away at their favorite couples' resort. They hiked, swam, got massages, relaxed, ate good food, and drank lots of margaritas. Most importantly, they reconnected as a couple. They continued to wrestle with whether or not they'd move to Capitol City and eventually decided they'd reevaluate after Kendall had done the commute for a few weeks.

Now it was Friday, Kendall's last day off. All week long she'd thought about what Jake had said about the importance of dealing with her growing resentment toward Nate.

That morning, she curled up in her prayer chair, opened her journal, and began writing.

Nate –

I'm guessing this letter will never see the light of day, but at the suggestion of my mentor, Jake, I'm going to write it anyway.

I've realized over the last few weeks that despite my best efforts to the contrary, I left a few things unsaid between us. For my own health, I need to say them.

First, Nate, I want to thank you. Thanks for the opportunity to serve the good people at Grace during these last three years. That part of my ministry was truly a privilege. Thanks for giving me the space to figure out who I am as a youth pastor. I've learned things here that I will carry with me into the future.

Thanks, Nate, for also finally recognizing my value and even for going to great lengths to show me that with your grand gesture.

But Nate, despite that, I also need to tell you how much you've hurt me during my time at Grace.

You've never had my back. Not once. The incident with Jill was your most egregious failure, but it was not the only one. I can list numerous other times when you sided with parents instead of me.

Now, I know that some of those times were probably deserved. I'm not completely innocent.

But you were my boss, Nate. You were supposed to have my back. You were supposed to give me a chance to explain. You were supposed to listen to my side of the story before drawing any conclusions about what had (or had not) happened. You never did that. You always just assumed that what someone told you was the truth. And maybe it was their truth, but it wasn't always mine.

At Grace, I never felt free to experiment because I always feared what would happen if I failed. Even though you only demanded my resignation once, I always feared you'd ask for it. Or worse yet, that you'd simply fire me and that my career in youth ministry would be over.

And here's something else, Nate. Do you realize that you never heard me teach or lead a discussion at Grace? In my three years there, you never once cared enough to come to The Lighthouse to see for yourself what was going on. In many ways, that's your loss. But it's also a loss for the kids. You might not realize this, but YOU are their pastor, Nate. The kids adore you, even though they don't know you. Actually, now that I'm saying this, maybe they adore you because they don't know you.

Nate, I had things I wanted to learn from you during my time at Grace. I think I have the gift of teaching. I know you do. I wanted to be your student, but you never allowed me to. Now, I find myself grieving that loss as well.

I don't need to stay in touch with you. In fact, I honestly hope we don't. But I need to know that if I run into you, we can say hi with no hard feelings.

For that reason, I need to say this, Nate. I forgive you. For all the ways you failed to teach me, I forgive you. For all the ways you failed to pastor me, I forgive you. For all the ways you failed to listen, I forgive you. For all the ways you failed to support me, I forgive you. For all the ways you failed to genuinely partner with me, I forgive you.

I forgive you, Nate.

And because I do, I can honestly say, I wish you and Grace well.

Kendall

■ ■ ■

FRIDAY, AUGUST 7: THE FIRST WEEK AT FIRST CHURCH

Kendall walked in the door after her first week on the job with a smile on her face. Frank was waiting for her, a margarita in each hand.

"I thought a celebration was in order," he motioned toward the sushi dinner he'd laid out on the island. "You survived your first week at First Church!"

"It's been quite a week, hasn't it?" responded Kendall with a grin.

"How does it feel to have your first week under your belt?" asked Frank.

"So good," replied Kendall.

It really had been. She'd spent the week meeting one-on-one with high school teens and their parents. She'd gotten to know them and asked questions about their experience of the youth ministry thus far. She'd learned a lot and so far, nothing had caught her totally off guard, which she was incredibly thankful for. What she was discovering about First Church all fit with the impressions she'd left the interview process with. That, in and of itself, felt like a win.

A highlight of her first week had definitely been working with Jo. As she expected, Jo seemed to understand her more than Nate ever had.

Even so, she felt as though she was still trying to figure Jo out. As she'd met with people, they'd repeatedly described Jo as "pastoral."

"Earth to Kendall," Frank said. "I feel like I lost you."

"You did," admitted Kendall. "I was just thinking about Jo. Everyone I've met with has described her as pastoral, but I'm still not sure what people mean when they say that."

"I can help with that."

"Oh?" questioned Kendall, curious.

"Yeah. That's how I'd describe Jo too."

"What?!" exclaimed Kendall. "How would you know that? You haven't even met her!"

"Actually," replied Frank with a grin, "I have."

"What?" Kendall was genuinely confused.

"Jo called me this morning and asked if we could grab a cup of coffee. I was a little taken aback, but I had a window in my calendar, so I said yes. I'm glad I did."

"You had coffee with my boss this morning?" asked Kendall, still trying to wrap her mind around that. "Where?"

"Here in Springfield!" replied Frank. "She actually drove forty minutes to have coffee with me!"

"Should I be alarmed?"

"No, not at all," replied Frank. "I almost said no to her because I didn't want to overstep. We've worked hard not to be seen as a two-for-one deal. I was concerned having coffee with Jo would violate that. I took a chance and told her that when she called. She assured me this wasn't what that was about. So, I went."

"What on earth did you guys talk about?" questioned Kendall, still not quite understanding what was going on. "You didn't say anything about me that's going to be problematic, did you?"

"No," replied Frank honestly. "That's the thing. We didn't talk about you at all."

"Really? That seems hard to believe."

"Really?" retorted Frank, starting to get defensive. "Contrary to popular belief, my entire life is *not* about you and your ministry, Kendall."

"I know," replied Kendall, frantically trying to retreat. "I didn't mean to imply that. It just seems strange that you met with my boss today and I didn't know about it. What *did* you guys talk about?"

"Me," said Frank. "She said she wanted to get to know me. She asked me lots of questions about my job, hobbies, and interests. She said she's seen firsthand from her own husband's experience how difficult it is for a guy to be a pastor's spouse and so she wanted to be proactive about getting to know me, for me."

"Really?" asked Kendall. "That's pretty incredible."

"It really is," agreed Frank. "Jo knows me more after one day than Nate knew me after three years. And get this. Jo's last question was, 'I know how hard it is being a pastor's spouse. How can I support you?' Imagine that. A pastor asked *me* how they could support me. I'm still astounded. In our entire married life, all pastors have ever asked me is how I can support them. But Jo asked me how she can support me. I feel known and cared for. If that's not pastoral, I don't know what is."

"Hmmm." Kendall was still not sure what to make of this all.

"I've got to tell you, Kendall," began Frank. "I honestly wasn't sure you'd made the right decision to come to First Church. But now, there's not a doubt in my mind. You chose right. Not only will you get to use all your gifts at First Church in ways that I really believe will transform all involved, but I think for the first time in our married life, we might actually be cared for as people. That means more to me than I ever imagined it would."

"Wow." Kendall was a bit unsure what else to say. After a beat, though, she found herself replaying Frank's words. "Wait a minute! You weren't sure I'd taken the right job and you didn't say anything? I don't know whether to laugh or cry about that. Aren't you supposed to let me know these things?"

"Well," said Frank, "I pushed you to take the job at Grace because Nate seemed so great during the interview process. Then I pushed you to go to Trinity only to discover Aaron's condescending attitude toward their neighbors. I kinda feel like I've lost all my credibility."

"My being at Grace was not your fault, babe," said Kendall, hoping to exonerate Frank for whatever guilt he seemed to be feeling. "And once we found out about Aaron's attitude, we *both* changed our minds about Trinity."

"I know. But still, despite what a fuss I made about your applying for jobs without telling me, ultimately, I wanted this to be your decision. It's your career, after all."

"But it's our church. We're team Kendall and Frank. We make these decisions together."

"I appreciate that, I do. But your job is weird because it blends career with our personal lives. I don't want to get in the way of your career."

"You never have," Kendall assured him. "You've only ever supported me. And I'm thankful for that. Just like I'm thankful for Jo and the way she reached out to you today. I think I've got a lot to learn from her…and unlike Nate, I think she wants to teach me."

"I think so, too," agreed Frank. "I don't know how long we'll be at First Church, but after your first week here I'm confident this is where God has called you. This is our next right thing."

"I'm so glad to hear you say that," replied Kendall.

"There's something else I need to tell you," said Frank. "Don't be mad okay?"

"I'll try," said Kendall hesitantly. "What is it?"

"I called a realtor today," confessed Frank.

"You did what?!?" cried Kendall, not sure whether to laugh or cry. "Weren't you the one who got upset with me for applying for jobs without talking to you first? Don't you think calling a realtor falls into that same category?"

"It does," admitted Frank. "But here's the thing. Despite my initial hesitation, like I said, I'm confident now that First Church is our next right thing. Jo's visit here today helped show me that. I know we said we'd reevaluate moving after you'd done the commute for a while. Well, you've done it for a few days and I already think there's no reason for us not to move…or at least look. I mean, as you reminded me, I can work from anywhere. So I asked Jo for a realtor recommendation and then called the person she recommended."

Kendall sat in stunned silence.

"Plus, it turns out my dream house is still available!" grinned Frank.

Kendall pulled Frank into a hug and laughed with joy.

■ ■ ■

SIX MONTHS LATER

Shortly after Kendall arrived at work, Jo called and asked if they could connect. "Sure," replied Kendall. "Want me to come down to your office?"

"No—give me five minutes and I'll come to yours."

Kendall hung up the phone, smiling. She was still floored by Jo's willingness to meet in her office. It was such a little thing, but it made her feel as though they were true partners, as though Jo was never angling for the upper hand.

A few minutes later, Jo arrived and sat down. They met weekly to update one another on life and ministry as well as collaborate about things they were working on in the future. Kendall looked forward to these times. Because they happened so frequently, she was not the least bit apprehensive about Jo requesting an additional meeting.

"I wanted to let you know that Tina Sannos called me yesterday," Jo said.

Kendall mentally sorted through her catalogue of parishioners, trying to place Tina.

"Tina is Chloe's mom," Jo clarified.

Chloe was one of the youth ministry's regulars, although Kendall wasn't sure why. She never seemed happy to be there and had turned down Kendall's repeated invitations for coffee.

"Apparently, Chloe isn't happy about the direction you're taking the youth ministry," Jo explained.

"What do you mean?" Kendall felt her heart sink to her stomach.

"Chloe seems to think you're doing several things wrong," replied Jo.

"Like what?" Kendall was now a nervous wreck.

"Let me see here," said Jo, pulling out a paper with notes. "First, you are *not* fun like Chad was. Second, you're using the Bible a little too much for Chloe's liking. Third, there are too many adults hanging around the youth group. Fourth, you're paying too much attention to the group's losers. Chloe is concerned First Church is about to lose its reputation as the coolest youth group in town."

Kendall honestly didn't know what to say. All these things were true. But quite honestly, they were all changes she was proud of. She *was* paying attention to the group's losers, although she preferred to think of them as the marginal kids. She thought that was what Christian community was supposed to entail. Plus, it was her gift of hospitality in action. There *were* more adults hanging around. They were the adult leaders she was carefully selecting and equipping for ministry. She knew she wasn't a teen magnet. She never had been. But what troubled her most was the comment about Scripture. How was she supposed to disciple kids without the Bible?

As Kendall sat wondering if she'd made a mistake of gargantuan proportion by coming to First Church, Jo continued. "I just wanted to let you know that based on my conversation with Tina and on our conversations over the last six months, I think you're doing *really* good ministry, Kendall."

"Really?" Kendall was unsure what else to say, and immediately thought about how different this conversation would have gone with Nate, who undoubtedly would have had Tina sitting in the room when he went to confront her about it.

"Really," Jo said. "If you're upsetting Chloe and Tina, you're doing something right."

"What do I need to do to make it right with them?" asked Kendall, still worried what the fallout from this would be.

"Nothing," said Jo.

"What?" questioned Kendall. "I know better than that. You can't just do nothing when a family calls and complains."

"At First Church you can," replied Jo. "Or actually, let me clarify. You can do nothing because I already handled it."

"What?" asked Kendall again, even though she felt as if she'd been saying the same thing for the last thirty minutes. "How did you handle it?"

"I told Tina about our conversations—both during your interview process and more recently. I informed her that we've asked you to build a ministry that's not centered on you, but that's instead centered on Jesus and that's run by a team of called and equipped leaders. I told her that we hired you to partner with parents in the discipling of our teens and that from what I've seen when I've visited your gatherings, you're doing an exceptional job at that. Then I asked Tina to give you a chance. If she won't do that, I can suggest some other area churches where she might be a better fit."

"You did not actually say that," said Kendall, convinced she'd heard Jo wrong.

"I did," said Jo. "And I'll say that to anyone else who calls to complain about you. Oh, don't get me wrong, Kendall. I'll listen to them. If I think their complaints have merit, I'll ask them to talk directly to you about them because I'm confident you'll receive that feedback well. But if it's meritless, I'll put a stop to it. I won't have Christians behaving badly toward one another in this congregation. You're too important to our ministry here."

"Wow," said Kendall. "I don't know what else to say."

"I expected that," said Jo. "And that's okay. Is there anything else we need to talk about right now?"

"Not at all," said Kendall.

"Well, then, I'll head back to my office. I know you've got a sermon to prepare for Sunday."

"I do," Kendall said, grinning. She was excited to be preaching in *big church* for the second time since she'd begun her ministry at First Church.

As Jo left her office, Kendall looked up at the framed print on her wall. It was a map of the Israelites' journey from Egypt to the promised land. Jake had given it to her as a gift shortly after she started at First Church.

"First Church isn't the promised land," he reminded her as she opened it. "But it's not Egypt, either."

Today, as she sat in awe of the conversation she'd just had with Jo, she couldn't help but think about where she'd been, and how glad she was to be where she was now. *First Church isn't perfect. It's not the promised land*, she thought. *But it is where I'm called. And that's enough.*

■ ■ ■